Life Is a
Long Song

A Compendium of
Jethro Tull
in 33 1/3 Songs

Richard Taylor

Life Is A Long Song

A Compendium of Jethro Tull in 33 1/3 Songs

Richard Taylor

WP
WYMER
PUBLISHING
Bedford, England

Contents

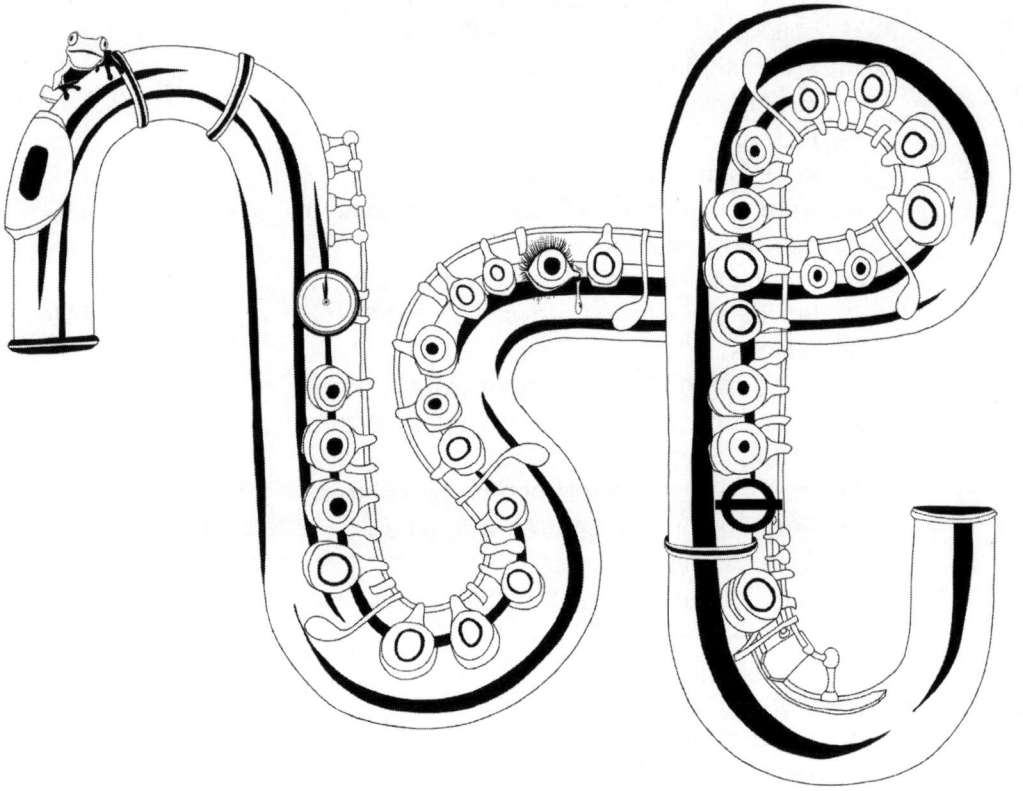

Acknowledgements

I was lucky to work with two wonderful artists, who drew the illustrations for each chapter in the book. They were Bekah Elliott and Elaine Tribley. I gave them the song titles with the taglines, and then suggested they listened to the song and looked at the lyrics.

After that, it was up to them and their creativity. Some of the illustrations are obvious in their link to the song, while others are weirdly obscure and are cognitively "interesting". This is quite right too!

Rather like an Ian Anderson Jethro Tull song lyric, it is good that some drawings are enigmatic, mysterious and challenging. This is, after all, "Prog Rock High Culture Art" we are talking about!

Hopefully as you look forward to reading the book, then what will happen with the drawings will also be eagerly anticipated.

****

I would like to thank my wife Linda for proofreading. One of my major hobbies is putting commas in the wrong place in text, so she had her work cut out. I would also like to apologise to her now, officially in print, for endlessly banging on about Jethro Tull and playing her all of Thick As A Brick "just one more time".

My friend Keith "Prog" Needham read the manuscript for content and in his wonderful "up north" Yorkshire way told me what was good and what was not so good. It has been a better book for your input, Keith!

I would very much like to thank Jerry Bloom at Wymer Publishing for giving me the fantastic opportunity to get this, my first book, published.

I have to mention, of, course Ian Anderson, Martin Barre and everyone else ever associated with the magical entity that is Jethro Tull, for providing me with the soundtrack of my life and just a little inspiration for this book!

Oh, nearly forgot... I am indebted to Gerald Bostock for aiding and abetting with regard to the Thick As A Brick chapter.

Introduction

Within the space of five months over 1971-72, two acoustic rock songs had been released, that had a profound effect on me. I was 16 in September 1971, a formative age, on the verge of a musical awakening and therefore ripe for change.

A year earlier when I was fifteen, I still did not understand or appreciate album orientated rock music. I had hated "Voodoo Chile" by Jimi Hendrix, even though it got bizarrely to number 1 for one week in the singles charts in the UK.

I did not get it when some of the boys in school brought in a copy of Led Zeppelin III with its circular rotating sleeve and talked enthusiastically about Jimmy Page and Robert Plant.

But then somehow and somewhere in mid-1971, it all changed for me. Maybe it was hormonal, maybe it was testosterone, maybe it was peer group pressure, but I began to hate pop music (I don't now).

Rock, initially in the form of Deep Purple, began to float my vote and boat. I distinctly remember at a party kissing a girl in time to Ritchie Blackmore's frantic guitar solo from "Child In Time". It was funny how the girl walked off and avoided me afterwards. I think she preferred to kiss somebody else to the sound of the New Seekers, and quite right too.

Even then, I liked a little light music throwing in a little dainty acoustic plucking, as well as the more bombastic rock pieces.

In early 1972, I heard Neil Young for the first time with the acoustic "Heart Of Gold". I loved everything about it and am still a huge fan to this day, but he is only my second favourite rock artist, and it is only my second favourite song of that time.

Five months earlier in September 1971, I had come across the first acoustic piece. I watched a video on *Top Of The Pops* of a long-haired man jumping up and down in the air in time to a song. He was holding a flute but did not appear to play it. He certainly did play for real in the song studio recording along with an acoustic guitar.

The song I discovered was "Life Is A Long Song" by a group

called Jethro Tull. The name Jethro Tull sounded so wonderfully weird and cool. I was hooked already. It was only years later that I realised the original Jethro Tull invented the agricultural seed drill in 1701 and was reincarnated in name only in 1968, as a rock group. Ian Anderson sang it as "Life Is A Longsong" it being difficult to separate the silent "g" from the more noisy "s" so longsong became one singing word. I loved that effect as well, to add to my smitteness.

The voice, acoustic guitar, strings and of course the meandering and descending unique selling point flute lines, all add to its beauty. To say that I loved this song would be an understatement. It's still in my top ten songs of all time and I never get tired of listening to it. It got to number 11 in the singles charts, so it was around simmering in my consciousness for some weeks.

You can find out more in the chapter on "Life Is A Long Song" further on. It could also be part of a book title, I wonder?

Unfortunately for my friends and long-suffering family, I have been addicted to Tull ever since. But why? Firstly, I love the chords, melodies and rhythms inherent in the songs. Tull are famous for being everything you could want musically (maybe not country, rap or soul) with hard rock, a hint of metal, soft rock, Celtic folk, classical, jazz and blues to the fore.

I also love the light, the shade and mix of electric instruments and acoustic music, where the Celtic Scottish folk influence in particular does it for me. I think "Dun Ringill" from the *Stormwatch* album really illustrates this type of Tull song. Could it be my favourite Tull song ever? Read on to find out.

Then there is the ubiquitous flute, absolutely everywhere in Tull song, history and mythology, all because Ian Anderson was never going to play the guitar like Eric Clapton.

They come in nickel, silver and gold metals, and sometimes they can be made of wood, especially bamboo. Ian has played mainly metal flutes on nearly every Tull song, apart from the mid-nineties, where, through World Music and Indian influences, he played a bamboo one quite a bit.

The song "Aqualung" is a rarity with no flute and of course it is famously ironic that Jethro Tull's most famous song does not have that instrument on it. It does have a great guitar solo though, more on which later.

There are Tull songs that use the flute for decoration like "Clasp" from *The Broadsword And The Beast*. Others are famous for the flute solo, where said instrument can out-riff and out-syncopate any guitar with heavy metal blowing as in "Locomotive Breath".

Finally, there are the tracks awash with so much flute, that you could drown in the trilling and go to heaven, such as with "Bourée".

In five-hundred years' time, a young astronaut on the Mars colony will say, "Do you remember Jethro Tull?" The reply from his Martian companion would be "Yes, they were the band with the flute player who stood on one leg".

Jethro Tull will not be remembered for prog rock meanderings, and just the usual guitar, keyboard, bass, drum instrumentation common to most rock groups.

Nor will future musicologists discuss love songs, debauched behaviour or makeup as pertaining to Jethro Tull. If ever a band had a "unique selling point" to make them different in the eyes of most people who are not super fans, then it is the flute and the man who played it, the unique Ian Anderson!

Any sensible examination of the life and times of the band that is Jethro Tull cannot downplay the many others who have been in the band and have made fantastic contributions to Tull, even if they do not play the flute (with one exception).

I hope to highlight these contributions. During the "In The End" chapter at the back of the book, I will come back to more comments about ex and present band members.

Of course, I have to mention the magnificent guitar-playing hero Martin Barre, who over forty-two years made a second only to Ian contribution to the band.

Although not quite up to Ian's standard, Martin could occasionally chip in with some of his own flute playing.

Meanwhile, being a clever sort of chap (sort of), I always love, appreciate and thoroughly understand all of Ian's wonderful lyrics. Er... no I don't, not all the time anyway. I struggle with lyrics generally and don't always get them.

Some of Tull's "yes it is, no it is not" lyrics I find tricky to follow. It always gets me thinking but does not quite give me the answer.

Considering that Ian has always encouraged fans to make their own minds up (and not to worry if they don't understand), he would probably be quite pleased about this.

However, if you want a challenge, analyse the lyrics to *A Passion Play*, and then those to *Tales From Topographic Oceans* by Yes. There is enough there to befuddle the greatest of all analytical minds.

Prog rock of the early seventies had a lot to answer for. That is something for you to ponder though, if you are bored in an afternoon. The analysis, therefore, of song lyrics in this book are open to dispute, debate and questioning, but hopefully, that will give you, the reader, something to think about and discuss in the Jethro Tull Universe.

My favourite lyrics are probably Ian's more romantic ones. At my wedding, best man Mike read out the lyrics to "Wondering Aloud" from the *Aqualung* album, a truly soppy but nice moment.

I love, and can appreciate, the great romantic lyrics from "Fire At Midnight" from the *Songs From The Wood* album. I also love the surreal words spoken and sung on "The Story Of The Hare Who Lost His Spectacles". Just don't ask me to explain the rest of *A Passion Play*!

I'm sure you can see why I thought that a little book-writing about Tull's songs might be fun activity to try. For this, the first thing I did was to find out just how many studio-recorded songs Jethro Tull have released.

I thought it would be easy: count the songs on the 23 studio albums so far, to start. But then there are additional tracks associated with each album, singles and their B-sides, and the odd additional track on compilation albums.

I have discounted live tracks, remastered and reworked versions. Before I give the figures, I must add a disclaimer here that they may not be entirely accurate.

Regard them as just a rough estimation to illustrate my points.

If you wish to sue for inaccuracies, can I point out I have no money and I have just left the building.

So here it goes: Jethro Tull has 264 studio recordings. Over Ian Anderson's solo albums are another 78 tracks making 348 in total, but I will concentrate on just the Tull tracks: 264.

By comparison, Elton John has put out 378 studio song recordings, The Who have 245, Led Zeppelin only has 92, but leading the way are, not surprisingly, The Rolling Stones with 422. My next book on the Stones that will be written later today will be a compendium in 78 songs — in line with the original vinyl speed that Mick, Keith and Ronnie will remember from their childhoods.

So, how many songs can represent a history of Tull? I could do a chapter on every song. At five-hundred words a song on average though, that would make a book of 132,000 words, a tome of epic proportions.

There is a chance I might die or go out to lunch before finishing, so a bit of a reduction is in order. It is fashionable in some books now to discuss the subject title in one hundred or fifty chapters, whether the book may be about people, football matches, train stations or gluten-free meals.

However, I thought a suitable original number for the aged Tull fan might be what?... How about 33 1/3 songs? This was the number of times per minute a vinyl album went round a record deck. 45 revs per minute were for singles, but of course, all you ancient Tullites out there will know this.

It is also a reasonable sample size in the end, to be a little representative of a large output band like Tull. It also seems a fun number to pick as it is linked to the traditional long-playing record or album; that was the predominant musical format available when Tull started in 1968.

What about the third of a song? Well, dear reader, you will have to wait until the end of the book for that choice, and I may need to be creative.

How will I choose the songs to do? 33 1/3 songs is about 12.5% of all JT's songs, so how can I represent all of Tull through a smallish sample size? One song track from each of the twenty-three Jethro Tull albums is a must.

The other tracks will consist of ones I absolutely love, and ones I find very interesting or even perplexing. Then there are the ones I just have to pick, otherwise Ian Anderson won't speak to me ever again, or no one will buy the book.

Album tracks then will be picked, along with singles,

additional tracks, and some songs with more than one version released in different time periods will be included.

They will come up in the book in more or less the chronological order in which they were released, but it can all get a bit confusing with box sets, unreleased tracks and brand-new versions.

I wish you the best of Tull luck when reading the fun chapter on "Jack-A-Lynn". There were seven versions of this song, eight if you include the karaoke song mentioned at the end of the chapter.

For each track, I will do some bits and bobs on the music and make some guesses about the lyrics. I will also try to pick out something unique about that track that lends itself to further discussion.

For example, in "Locomotive Breath" it might be how many times it has been played live in comparison to other classic rock songs of a similar age.

For the 1969 single "Living In The Past", it could be some analysis on the use of different time signatures in popular songs, while for "Pibroch (Cap In Hand)" from *Songs From The Wood*, I have talked about the use or non-use of bagpipes in rock and pop music (a Pibroch is a composition for Bagpipes).

I will also talk round the song to explain what was happening in "the where, the when, the how and why" with Tull and the band members at that time. I also give a score out of ten for each song, as I am a bit sad that way, what with being a retired teacher.

As on popular television shows, it will hopefully generate a fun debate as to just how badly I score either up or down. It will become a Strictly Come Tull workout, without the sequins.

It is important to state now that this is not a conventional historical biography of Jethro Tull. That is covered in several other excellent books that I have copies of; some of which will be mentioned in the bibliography at the very end.

If you want a "recording, tour, band change in formation over the years", chronological account, then those books are your baby.

This book, however, is a compendium; a collection of precise, detailed information essays on a particular subject – in this case in its 33 1/3 chapters on the 33 1/3 songs. My writing style will hopefully be informative, entertaining and quirky.

While this book is about Jethro Tull, there is a little bit of me in the writing. I hope to bring out some of the more surreal links that some Tull songs suggest to me, that just maybe no one else has thought of and are not present in other Tull books.

There might be a very good reason for this, of course. However, with this in mind, I have added a tagline for each song (as you will have seen in the contents page).

The taglines give a clue as to where the content of that chapter might be heading. The book will show all this in the best possible light and taste, or it will show that I am quite mad. You can decide.

It is time for a quick word on the use of the words "song" and "track" in the book.

"Track" is used exclusively for "Bourée", The Pine Marten's Jig" and "Dharma For One" version (1) as they are all instrumentals.

Then, to some extent, the words become interchangeable, so I do not get too repetitive with one word or another. However, as a general rule I use the word "track" to talk about the instrumentation for the song, and the word "song" for the singing lyrical part of the track. There, that is nice and clear.

At home, as already indicated, I have a copious amount of Tull books. I also have box sets, magazines and have searched the Internet to be as accurate as possible with Tull facts throughout.

Naturally, any errors here will almost certainly be the fault of the proofreader.

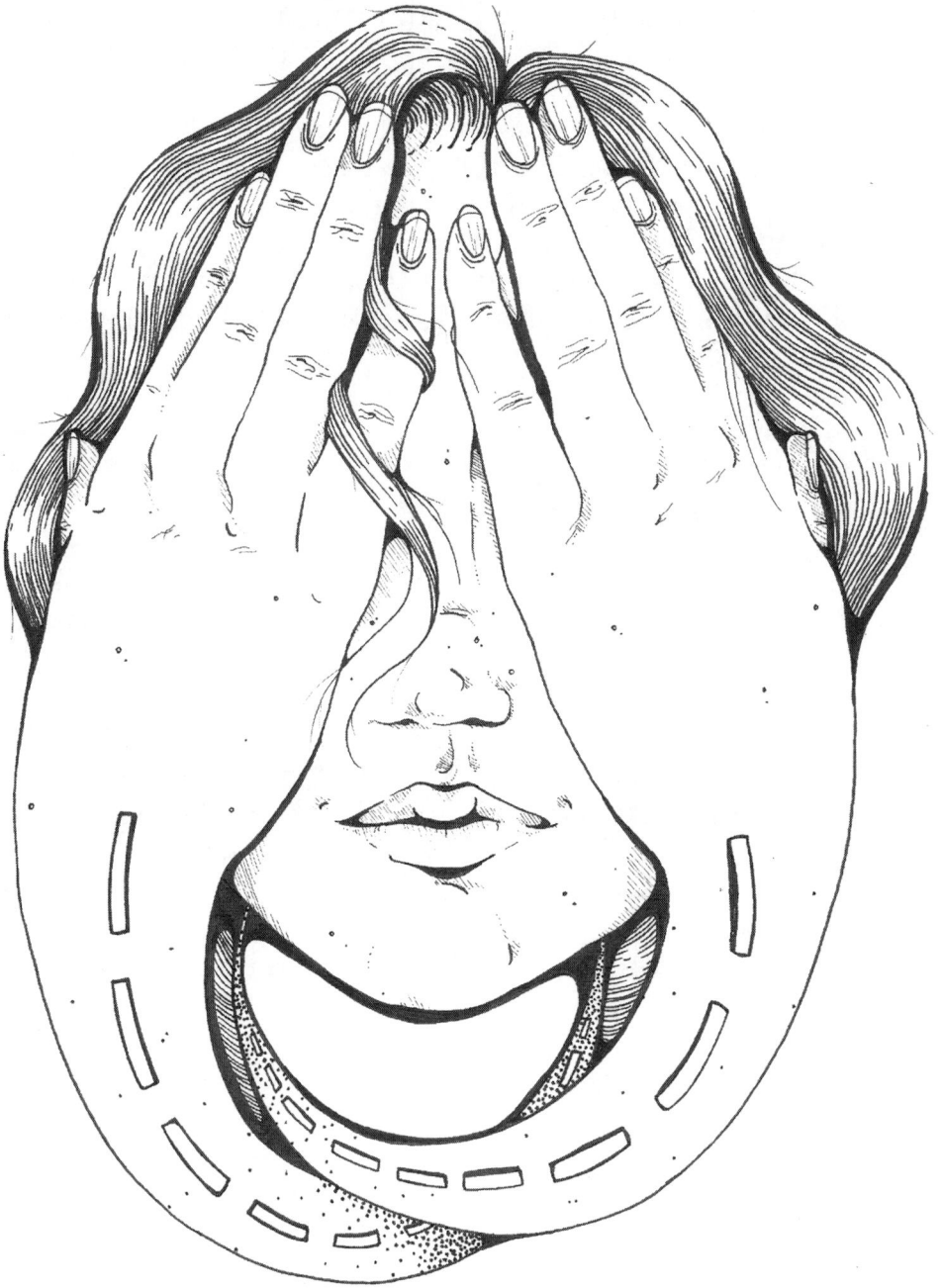

1.
Song For Jeffrey
Our heroes burst onto the scene

Meanwhile, back in the year... 1968. From the remnants of the John Evan Band and the Blades came the prototype, misspelled Jethro Toe. This name only lasted briefly, giving way to over fifty years of the real Jethro Tull.

Ian Anderson was on vocals, flute, and harmonica, often while standing on one leg. Mick Abrahams played guitar in a blues style reminiscent of Eric Clapton.

Glenn Cornick was on bass (soon to be with headband), and Clive Bunker played drums with syncopated power.

Their first single, released in early 1968 on the MGM label, was "Sunshine Day" written by Mick, backed by "Aeroplane" by Ian and Glenn Barnard (Cornick).

The single was erroneously credited to Jethro Toe on the central record label. It's just as well this name didn't stick!

The band were impoverished, living in bedsits in London, surviving on tinned soup and putting ten shillings (50p) in the electricity meter to keep the lights on.

They began playing regular gigs at the Marquee in London, booked and supported by owner John Gee. They caught the attention of Terry Ellis and Chris Wright of Chrysalis Records, who offered them a record deal in June 1968.

Their big live moment came at the 8th Sunbury National Jazz and Blues Festival on the 10th of August 1968, when the lunatic long-haired flute player became the dominant personality on stage.

When not performing, Ian Anderson was and is quiet,

reflective, and deep-thinking.

On stage, there was competition to unseat Mick Abrahams as the bandleader. Ian's breathy, expiratory flute playing, while standing on one leg and leaping onto the other, went down a storm and became their unique selling point.

Jethro Tull became known as the band with the "heavy metal instrument", the flute. That's not to say that Mick, Glenn, and Clive were not brilliant at the festival — they were a great live band. It was at Sunbury where our heroes burst onto the scene.

Expectations were high when Jethro Tull began recording their first album between June and August 1968.

"Song For Jeffrey", written by Ian, was played on John Peel's Top Gear in early September 1968 and released as a single in the UK on 27th September 1968, backed by "One For John Gee" written by Mick.

Despite the anticipation, the record failed to make an impact on the charts. The song was later included in the album *This Was*, which was released on 25th October 1968.

"Song For Jeffrey" is three minutes and twenty-two seconds long and can be described as a bouncy, psychedelic Delta blues number featuring slide guitar, harmonica, and breathy, jazzy, bluesy flute.

Lyrically, as was typical of the time; it is strange and enigmatic. The subject, poor young Jeffrey, had "ceased to see where I'm going".

Does Ian's idiosyncratic friend need a push in the right direction? Or did Jeffrey, like the hare in chapter 11, perhaps just need new spectacles?

Jeffrey was Jeffrey Hammond, the son of parents who coincidentally shared the same surname before marriage.

When Jeffrey joined Jethro Tull, he naturally adopted the name Jeffrey Hammond-Hammond, incorporating both his parents' original surnames. It's a good thing Ian never tried to fit all that into a song!

Jeffrey was a school friend of Ian's who, by 1968, was in art school and became the subject of three Tull songs: the aforementioned "Song For Jeffrey", "Jeffrey Goes To Leicester Square" from *Stand Up* (1969), and "For Michael Collins, Jeffrey and Me" from *Benefit* (1970).

Jeffrey became Tull's bass player in late 1970, replacing Glenn Cornick, whom Ian considered too unfocused and hedonistically "rock 'n' roll".

Glenn went on to form Wild Turkey, which achieved only modest success.

As a character, Jeffrey was eccentrically artistic, urbane, wittily weird, and endearingly entertaining. He, along with Ian and John Evan, wrote the Pythonesque "Story Of The Hare Who Lost His Spectacles" on *A Passion Play*.

Notably, Jeffrey is one of the few rock bass players to be immortalised in song three times before having even joined the band. He eventually left Tull in 1975 to return to his first love, painting.

By late 1968, the writing was on the wall for Mick Abrahams. Due to musical or personal differences, or perhaps both, he either left of his own accord or was fired from Jethro Tull, depending on which account could be on the right side of history.

Like Jeffrey, Mick was supposedly immortalised in song by Ian on "Fat Man" from *Stand Up* in 1969. The physically circumspect Mick then went on to form another three-syllable band, Blodwyn Pig, which achieved considerably less success.

But boy, could he play guitar! Check out any of Mick's playing on the Internet, especially on "Cat's Squirrel" from *This Was*.

Steve Howe (future Yes) and Davey O'List (The Nice) were contenders for the Tull guitar gig. A left-handed guitarist from a Birmingham band called Earth was also in the running.

This brings us to a truly bizarre alternative universe where Tony Iommi became Tull's new guitarist after Mick left, stayed with Tull for forty years, and the band was renamed Jethro Sabbath in 1970.

Not quite, of course, but Tony did join Tull for a few weeks at the end of 1968. He soon decided that insane flute players were not for him and started Black Sabbath, who you may have heard of (rumour has it they never had a flute player).

Tony played with Tull during their performance at the Rolling Stones *Rock & Roll Circus* in December 1968, miming Mick Abrahams' guitar part in "Song For Jeffrey".

Glenn Cornick doubled-up, miming harmonica and bass,

while Ian played live for both vocals and flute.

Martin Barre soon joined the band and played Mick's guitar parts live for over forty years, including "Song For Jeffrey" whenever it appeared on various tours.

I discovered Jethro Tull in 1971 with "Life Is A Long Song" (see chapter 9) and fell in love with that pesky flute.

This led me to regress in time to discover "Song For Jeffrey" from 1968. I loved its jerky rhythm, the contrast between harmonica and flute, and the discombobulated, distant vocals (similar to "Aqualung" — see that chapter for details).

Even Mick's guitar was shimmering and sliding to great effect. It's a great mid-to-high-range Tull track with early flute as the unique selling point.

"Song For Jeffrey" is an excellent starting point for Jethro Tull, as it showcases all the key elements that hint at the band's future potential. The song features weird, enigmatic lyrics, and tight unison between bass, guitar, and drums, while Ian Anderson plays two instruments and sings. It's a quintessential early Tull song, earning a 6.5 out of 10 from me.

2.
Dharma For One
The Claghorn and the drum

Two tracks, but one piece of music: one instrumental and one song. One was a studio recording, while the other was a live extravaganza, released separately three years apart. It might sound confusing, but here's the breakdown:

There was "Dharma For One" (1) and "Dharma For One" (2). Version (1) was a studio instrumental, while version (2) featured additional lyrics and a slightly different musical arrangement. It was recorded live and released on record.

"Dharma For One" (1) was recorded in June 1968, along with the other tracks for *This Was*, and released in October 1968.

It was credited to both Ian and Clive Bunker and featured a drum solo. It was one of four instrumentals on the album. The others were "Serenade For A Cuckoo", featuring the flute, "Cat's Squirrel", showcasing guitar hero licks from Mick Abrahams, and "Round", featuring contributions from everyone, including manager Terry Ellis, who was likely counting his royalties to the music's beat.

"Dharma For One" (1) is a jaunty piece with all members giving it their all until 1:09, where an unusual sound, resembling a strangulated duck, emerges.

This is the infamous and entirely unique Claghorn, crafted from the body of a recorder, the bell of a trumpet, and the mouthpiece of a saxophone, which Ian plays from 1:09 to 1:28 — just nineteen seconds to etch its place in Jethro Tull legend.

Despite extensive research across books, magazines, and Internet forums, I still cannot find the definitive answer as to who invented the Claghorn, as both Jeffrey Hammond and Ian Anderson have claimed its creation.

I'll leave them to settle that debate among themselves. The track then transitions to Clive's drum solo, followed by some nifty guitar work by Mick, concluding in four minutes and sixteen seconds.

"Dharma For One" (2) was recorded live at the Carnegie Hall concert in 1970 and released on the *Living In The Past* album in 1971.

Frankly, this version surpasses (1) and is stunningly wonderful. Not only is it over twice as long as "Dharma For One" (1), but it also became a song, as Ian wrote lyrics for it.

Dharma, a theme present in Hinduism, Buddhism, and Sikhism, represents the order and custom that make life and the universe possible. Ian's lyrics suggest that Dharma may eventually come, but each person must find their own path — it may not be for everyone.

As was typical with Ian's lyrics around this time, they offer glimpses into universal truths, only to pull away at the last minute, leaving the listener to make their own interpretations. These were quintessentially enigmatic Jethro Tull lyrics, especially from around 1970.

The song navigates through various phases, almost foreshadowing the watershed of progressive rock in the 1970s. In the pursuit of Dharma-esque order and custom, the song features different movements, parts, and timings:

1. John Evan kicks off with a Hammond organ intro lasting twenty-eight seconds, leading to a dazzling instrumental section propelled by Clive's dynamic drums, racing along at 100 mph until the 1:15-minute mark when vocals emerge, continuing until 2:11 minutes.
2. Then begins the chanting of "Dharma, Dharma, Dharma."
3. At the three-minute mark, the whole band launches into a frenetic section led by amplified guitar, organ, and flute — a veritable freak-out. Although it feels like the band is playing at different speeds, the sheer dynamism and enthusiasm of the performance overcome any timing difficulties.

4. At 4:26, the first instrumental section concludes, followed by a return of vocals.
5. At 5:22, a monumental drum solo unfolds — an acquired taste for some, prompting readers and listeners to perhaps take a break for a bathroom visit or to make tea (but don't worry, Clive won't know).
6. The drum solo, always interesting, varied, exciting, and slightly dangerous, reaches its climax. Clive even appears to head-butt the cymbals, as witnessed on the Isle of Wight DVD from 1970, where "Dharma"'s arrangement was similar.
7. The drum solo concludes at 8:20, followed by a brief full-band interlude until 9:01 minutes.
8. Then, a short drum breakette extends to 9:30, leading into a full-band crescendo that carries through to the end at 10 minutes.

"Dharma For One" (1) has been performed live over the years in its original form, with Ian claiming to play the Claghorn during the appropriate section. However, more often than not, a variation of "Dharma For One" (2) has been played, which includes vocals but excludes the chants, essentially becoming a sort of "Dharma For One" (3) version.

Doane Perry, Tull's longest-serving drummer in the eighties, nineties, and 2000s and a huge fan of Clive Bunker, would often be called upon to complete the solo in seconds or less than a minute, as drum solos went out of fashion, while playing "Dharma". Nevertheless, it still worked well; Doane was and is a powerhouse drummer.

I love both versions of this song. "Dharma For One" (1) would score 8/10. However, "Dharma For One" (2) in all its myriad forms and with all its variations, with long or short drum solos over the years live, would score a resounding pounding 10/10.

3.
Living In The Past
Only dance to this when drunk

The theme tune for *Mission Impossible* cleverly begins with two long notes followed by two short notes, mimicking Morse code for "dash, dash" and then "dot, dot", representing an "M" and an "I" for "Mission Impossible". How clever is that?! This ingenious arrangement was possible because the composer, Lalo Schifrin, utilised a 5/4 time signature.

In contrast, the majority of modern pop music songs employ a 4/4 time signature, where the first beat of the bar is the most prominent, followed by this emphasis being repeated every fourth beat.

While there may be more technical aspects to 4/4 time, it's easy to grasp when I play air drums!

This time signature is synonymous with foot-tapping, head-banging, danceable rhythms that are consistently regular. Many classic rock songs, such as AC/DC's "Back In Black" and ZZ Top's "Gimme All Your Loving," are prime examples of tracks that flawlessly utilise the 4/4 time signature throughout.

However, 5/4 time signature offers more complexity and intrigue, particularly if you aspire to create artful, avant-garde, jazzy, or progressive music. Dave Brubeck's "Take 5" from 1959, as its name suggests, was in 5/4 time.

More recently, Taylor Swift's "Tolerate It" (2020) also employs this time signature. The Gorillaz, a cartoon band, boldly titled one of their tracks "5/4", featuring guitars in 5/4 time while the drums kept a 4/4 rhythm. This is where things start to become confusing for me.

Like trying to comprehend Einstein's Theory of Special

Relativity or some of Ian Anderson's lyrics, grasping time signatures can be challenging.

For instance, "Money" by Pink Floyd is in 7/4 time, although Roger Waters and Dave Gilmour argue it should be played as 7/8.

"Golden Brown" by The Stranglers alternates between 12/8 and 13/8 time signatures, despite the initial impression of a 3/4 waltz time.

The Beatles contributed a John Lennon-written track to the *White Album* (1968) titled "Happiness Is A Warm Gun," which featured four distinct song fragments, each with different time signatures: 2/4, 4/4, 5/4, 3/8, 9/8, 10/8, and a single bar of 12/4 to conclude.

It's a remarkable feat to incorporate such variety into a song lasting only two minutes and forty-three seconds.

Jethro Tull are, of course, renowned for their experimentation with weird and wonderful time signatures over the years, although perhaps not as intricate as this Beatle composition. However, they did venture into the realm of complexity right from their first single. It all began in 1969 when Ian was "ordered" to write a hit single.

In February 1969, Jethro Tull found themselves between albums, transitioning from *This Was* to *Stand Up*, while touring the USA.

During a mini-residency at the Boston Tea Party in mid-February, Ian accepted a £5 bet from manager Terry Ellis to write a hit single. Legend has it that he accomplished this feat in just one hour, holed up in a hotel room.

Thus, "Living In The Past" was born. Shortly thereafter, it was recorded in New Jersey, USA, and released as a single on 14th May 1969, reaching number 3 on the UK charts.

It was later re-released as a single in the USA in 1972 to promote the *Living In The Past* compilation album, reaching number 11 on the Billboard chart.

Glenn kicks things off with a punchy bass line, followed by the entrance of two flutes from Ian, accompanied by Martin and Clive on guitar and drums.

The song's richness is further enhanced by string instrumentation from the New York Symphony Orchestra.

Lyrically, there are "in and out" references to revolution and protest, reminiscent of John Lennon's two versions of The Beatles' "Revolution".

Personally, I absolutely adore this song; it's incredibly catchy. And, of course, it's renowned for being in 5/4 time!

Why would anyone attempt to write their first hit single in 5/4 time? But then this is Ian Anderson we are talking about!

Whether it was deliberate or accidental, the use of the wonky, jerky, swingy 5/4 time really pushes the track along.

Initially, it seemed unlikely that this song would become a hit, but it defied expectations. Its wonky, jerky, swingy rhythm surprisingly works! However, it's virtually impossible to dance to unless you're drunk!

In live performances over the years, there have been several great versions of the song, often with keyboard domination, especially in the eighties during Peter-John Vitesse's time, or as a flute and guitar workout led by Ian and Martin.

Although Ian has occasionally claimed during live shows that he doesn't like this song, I think that's just a wind-up.

I do wonder why there are so many great Tull tracks like this that I can listen to forever and not get bored. I have been listening to this track for only fifty-three years, since 1971, when I discovered Tull.

It could just be me or it could be the writing, arranging and playing by the genius of Ian Anderson and Jethro Tull. (Spoiler alert: if you think I am getting too soft in my Tull worship at this early stage in the book, then there is a famous song to come that I don't like anymore and don't play much, but this is not it).

It's a resounding Strictly Come Tull 10 from me for "Living In The Past".

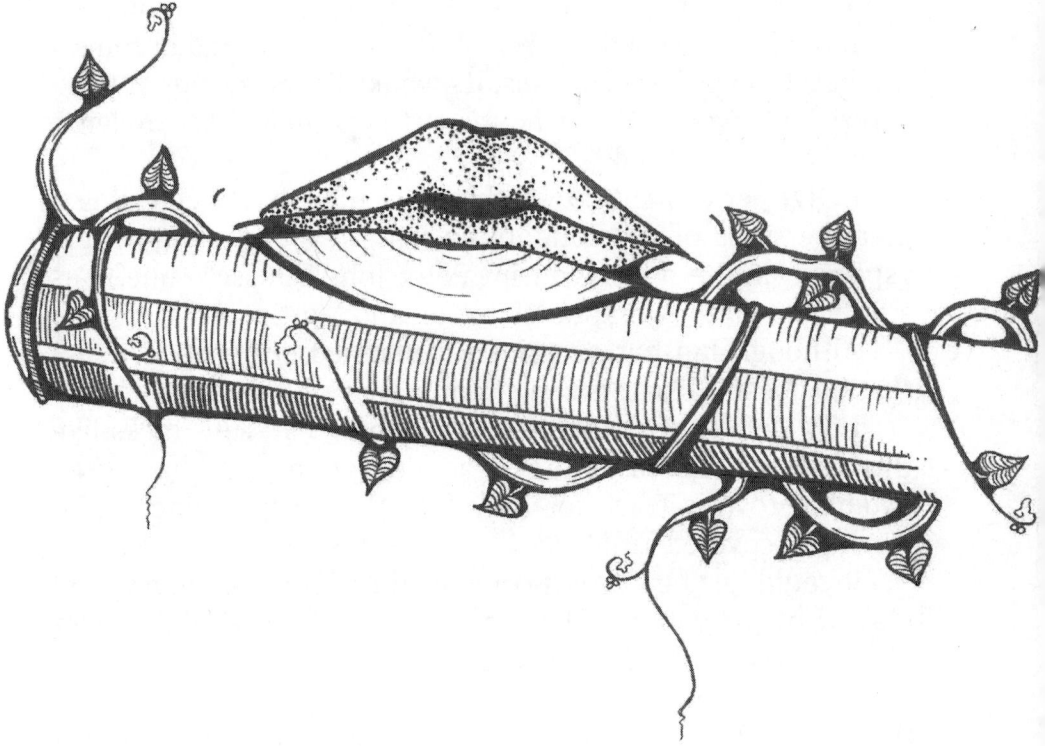

4.
Bourée
Where the flute player takes off on one leg

B ack in the 1700s, J.S. Bach composed "Suite No. 1 for Lute in E Minor", based on the Bourrée (note the two 'r's), a form of stylised dance pioneered by Louis XIV in France in the 1660s.

The lute, with its twenty-five strings, is quite challenging to play. Over time, the suite was adapted for the more accessible six-string acoustic classical guitar, becoming a popular piece for aspiring superstar classical players to practice.

By 1967, Ian Anderson was trying to keep up with Eric Clapton on his Fender Stratocaster. However, he realised he couldn't quite match up as a lead electric guitar player against the likes of Clapton, Jeff Beck, Jimmy Page, and Jimi Hendrix.

There's an unsubstantiated rumour that Ian sold his guitar to fellow Blackpoolian Lemmy, who would later gain fame with Motörhead.

In reality, Ian traded it in at a music shop for a heavy metal instrument — the flute. This nickel instrument, with its shiny silver coat, became the unique selling point of Jethro Tull's fame and fortune.

By late 1967, Ian could only produce a G note on the flute, but by mid-1968, when Tull recorded *This Was*, his playing had advanced to improvisations around blues scales.

Over in the USA in 1968, there was a well-known jazz musician, Roland Kirk, who was able to play two saxophones at the same time as a party trick. He was also useful on the clarinet and played the flute in a breathy vocalised style, which became a source of huge inspiration for Ian.

"Serenade To A Cuckoo" by Roland was covered as an instrumental on *This Was*. For the next album, *Stand Up*, Ian wanted a new instrumental to showcase his adaptation of Kirk's jazzy, breathy, vocalised flute playing for both the album and live performances.

Ian was living in a bedsit in Luton, and as Tull mythology has it, a music student in the similar apartment below him frequently practiced Bach's "Bourrée" on an acoustic guitar.

This caught Ian's attention. He mentioned his Bach encounter to Martin Barre, who then revealed that he had the sheet music for the piece. Thus, the stage was set for the recording of one of the most iconic Jethro Tull tracks of all time.

Around this time, it seems that Bach's influence extended to other musicians. In 1969, the band Bakerloo, featuring future Coliseum and Humble Pie guitarist Clem Clempson, released a track called "Drivin' Bachwards", which incorporated elements of Bourrée.

Additionally, it has been suggested that "Blackbird", a song written by McCartney for The Beatles' *White Album* in 1968, was also heavily influenced melodically by "Bourrée".

Personally, I don't hear that connection upon listening.

Minus the extra 'r', titled "Bourée", Tull's track was recorded around April 1969. It came out on *Stand Up* in August 1969.

As a single, it failed to make an impact in the UK but reached number 5 on the Dutch singles charts, where teenagers appreciated its classical flair.

Clocking in at three minutes and fifty-three seconds, it's a whirlwind of musical flautist mayhem with added drum and bass.

Virtually every Tull concert has included a rendition of "Bourée" in some form or another. Often, Martin would play the second counter flute melody at both the beginning and end of the track.

In later years, a classical-style introduction, featuring a slightly rearranged fluty bit from Ian, would precede the song.

This version is featured on *The Jethro Tull Christmas Album*, where Andy Giddings covers the second flute counter melody on the piano accordion.

Should "Bourée" be on a Christmas album? I'm not sure; it's an interesting juxtaposition to think of Santa, mince pies, and the Christmas spirit while listening to it.

Additionally, the 1969 original featured a notable and very nice mini bass solo by Glenn, which is absent in the Christmas version.

The mystery of the missing 'r' in "Bourée" remains. On the *Stand Up* album cover, "Bourée" is credited to Ian Anderson. Perhaps this was deemed acceptable since "Bourée" had lost the 'r', whereas "Bourrée" was obviously part of a J.S. Bach composition.

Fortunately, later copies corrected this by attributing it to "J.S. Bach, arranged by Ian Anderson."

In a similar vein, one might ponder if "Hotel California" should have been credited as "Ian Anderson, arranged by The Eagles". For more on this curious supposition, please see chapter 5.

I have been listening to "Bourée", both studio and live versions, for over fifty years and I still love it! Martin strums a few gentle chords only, but will get to become a guitar hero in chapter 5.

Glenn gets his solo, but apart from Ian, the other standout performer is Clive, who delivers some of the most incredible syncopated swing-style drumming. In my opinion, this is the best drumming he ever did with Tull.

It is a 10/10 from me and just might be in my top 3 Tull tracks of all time.

5.
Back To The Family
Where the guitar player gets to settle and weave in

At fifty-three seconds into "Back To The Family", Martin Barre begins with an open chord played from bottom to top, followed by a sequence of relentless, harsh power chords that serve as a backdrop to Ian's lyrics and flute solo.

At 3:08, there is an incredible interplay between Martin and Ian as their guitar and flute solos intertwine and diverge from each other. This marked the first time on a Tull record that Martin Barre and Ian Anderson were able to call and respond with their instruments together. Welcome to the show, Martin Barre!

When Mick departed, Ian sought a player who wasn't fixated on the blues, was open to experimentation, and wasn't a hardcore rock 'n' roll enthusiast (and definitely wasn't joining Black Sabbath!)

Martin had been performing with various soul cover bands, primarily on saxophone and flute with a bit of guitar thrown in, but he attended the Tull audition more out of hope than expectation. Initially rejected, he wasn't forgotten, and his second audition led to him practicing with Ian on Christmas Day in 1968.

He officially joined and performed live for the first time at the Penzance Winter Gardens on 30th December. Thus, Martin became an official member of Tull on the penultimate day of 1968.

Martin himself has been self-deprecating about his playing in 1969 with Tull, but in my humble opinion, his performances at that time were sensational. Just listen to "A New Day Yesterday", "Nothing Is Easy", and, of course, "We Used To Know", all from *Stand Up*, where Martin's best licks were later adopted by Don Felder and Joe Walsh for the guitar solos in the Eagles' "Hotel California".

The Eagles' chart-topper shares a similar chord structure and guitar solos with "We Used To Know" (though lacking the flute solo in "HC").

Ian has always claimed that "Hotel California" was a superior song to "We Used To Know", but I still believe Martin deserves royalties from the Eagles for his contribution to their success. Being a modest and kind-hearted person, Martin would likely feel embarrassed by such comparisons and my comments.

On "Back To The Family" I just love Martin's playing in how the guitar interplays with Ian's flute. Check the meshing and weaving in the outro on "Weathercock" from *Heavy Horses*, or "Rock Island" from *Rock Island* (both songs come up in later chapters).

Martin always plays for the song and with the song, not through the song or in spite of the song. There could never be a better guitar player for Tull!

"Back To The Family" was released on the *Stand Up* album in 1969. The original version was three minutes and forty-eight seconds long, while a longer version of three minutes and fifty-four seconds is available on the Steven Wilson box set remixes.

Additionally, a live version from Stockholm on 9th January 1969, at just over four minutes long, is included. Since then, Tull hasn't played it live too often, which is unfortunate.

However, in 2023, Martin occasionally performed the song live with his own band.

Lyrically, it's a sad song. Poor young Ian would get tired of being the rock star, go back to the family for a break, then get fed up and "go back to town for more action", but then get fed up again when the phone never stopped ringing. It's a no-win song in that regard. I am (not always) sure there was not a hint of the biographical from Ian here.

Anyway, I wanted to highlight this track for its unique

collaboration between Ian and Martin, featuring merry instrumental weaving interludes. In addition to Ian and Martin, drummer Clive's pounding rhythms and Glenn's walking, talking bass line also make great contributions.

For most people, this song would not make it into their top 51 Tull tracks, but after all these years I still really enjoy listening to it. It is a 9/10 for me, even on a bad hair day!

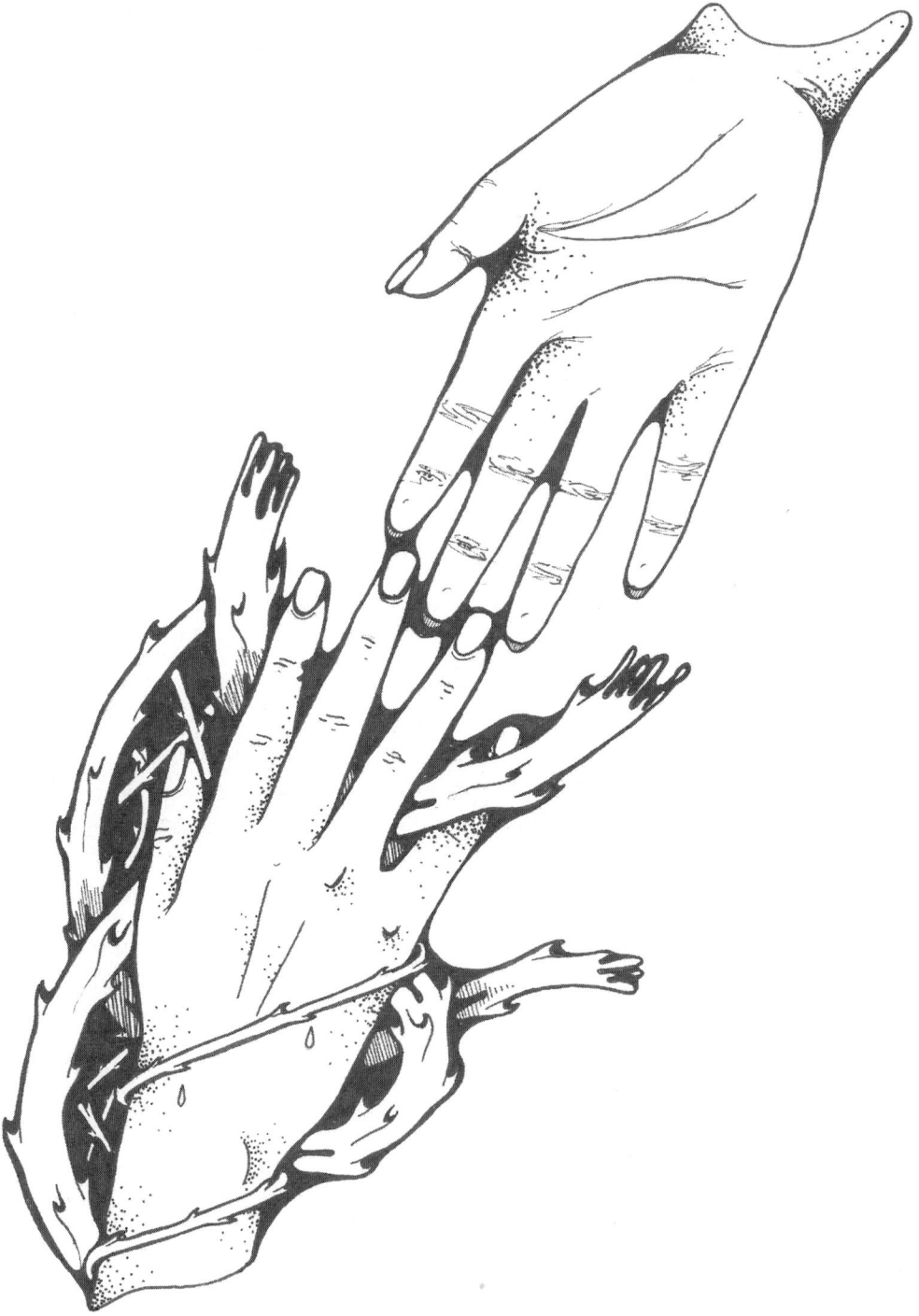

© Bekah Elliott

6.
With You There To Help Me
"By Kind Permission Of"

Jethro Tull's new keyboard player, John Evan, was born Evans but evolved into Evan as a 70s rock star, much like Keith (Richards) Richard of The Rolling Stones. Having an 's' at the end of your name just wasn't "rock 'n' roll" in the Tull and Stones families.

John had attended Blackpool Grammar School at the same time as Ian, who had migrated from Scotland with his family. Their shared interest in music led Ian to play guitar while John played a snare drum during their formative years at school.

Fortunately for Tullites everywhere, John, with his considerable talent for the piano, opted to switch to keyboards.

By 1969, John was pursuing a Pharmacy degree in London but was living in the same block of bedsits as Ian. For Tull's third album, Ian wanted to broaden the sound, and John was able to assist with some of the tracks as a session musician in January 1970, including "With You There to Help Me".

By April, John had joined the band full-time and played his first gig on 9th April in Nuremberg, West Germany.

In May 1970, the *Benefit* album was released, including our featured song. However, live performances of "With You There to Help Me" had evolved into something else of classical proportions, showcasing John's talent on par with Emerson and Wakeman.

"By Kind Permission Of" was a ten-minute virtuoso

showpiece arranged and played on piano by John, with interjected flautist help from Ian.

It referenced several classical composers, including Beethoven, Satie, and Rachmaninoff, and had hints of Gershwin, as well as jazzy blues elements. This track appeared on side 3, track 1 of the *Living In The Past* double LP in 1971, taken from a live recording at Carnegie Hall in New York in 1970.

"With You There To Help Me" also features separate guitar and flute solos. Ian's flute solos were recorded backwards, a quirky detail he would often humorously reference live by playing with his back to the audience, whilst maintaining his signature one-legged stance, of course.

Coming in at six minutes and eighteen seconds, it stands as Tull's longest studio track up to that point.

However, some might argue that the guitar and flute solos are overdone and too lengthy. The song seems to flutter and evaporate at the end, neither fading out nor stopping abruptly.

If this track were a bit shorter, perhaps "The Witch's Promise", the single from early 1970 on which John also played, could have been included on *Benefit*.

Lyrically, "With You There To Help Me" was a plea to Ian's first wife Jennie, who would keep the home fires burning until his return from gruelling tours, and be his support system.

Ian's approach to love songs has never been quite conventional, and this track is no exception. The lyrics carry a double meaning, offering a blend of overt romance and enigmatic undertones, as is typical of Ian's style.

I like this song, and it is probably the fan favourite from *Benefit*. However, I can never quite separate it from "By Kind Permission Of", which always followed it live in 1970.

On its own, "With You There To Help Me" gets a 6/10 from me. But when combined with "By Kind Permission Of", it quickly jumps to a 9/10.

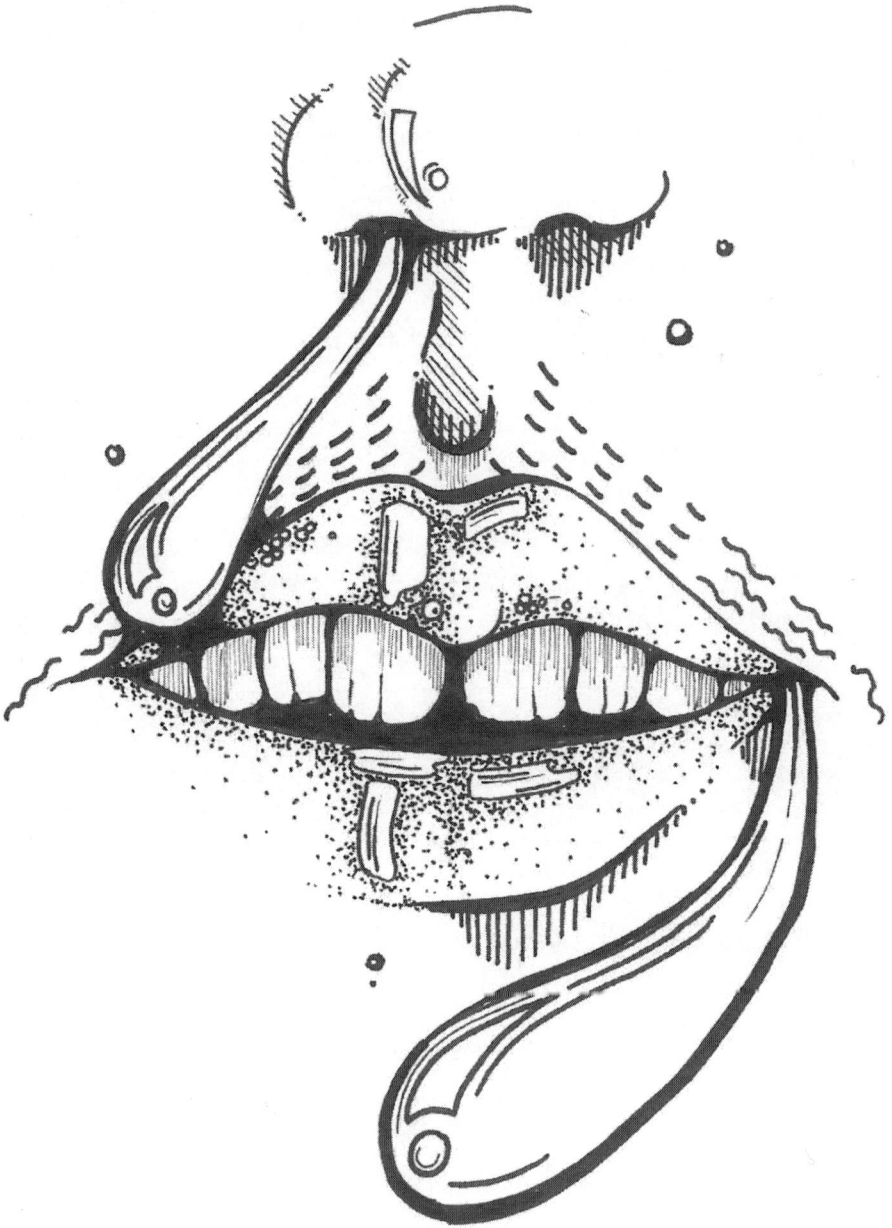

44

7.
Aqualung
The riff!

J ethro Tull's most famous song goes something like this: Duh, duh, duh, duh, duuuuh, duh. That is the famous starting riff. Next, a riffy power chord workout with vocals takes place (where is the flute?). Then an acoustic guitar joined by a piano with discombobulated vocals occurs (where is the unique selling point flute?).

Then the iconic famous (Jimmy Page-inspired) guitar solo blasts out (still no flute, this is getting to be a worry). Then a da, da vocal acoustic piece wanders in. It is all finished off with more riffy power chords and vocalising (and there is still no flute, for f***'* sake!).

The song, in case you may not have guessed, is "Aqualung", up there with other epics like "Stairway To Heaven" and "Smoke On The Water" as rock classics. Yet it contains no signature flute at all from Ian. What was he thinking?

My feeling is that Ian knew he had written a classic, knew he would be remembered for his flute-playing and deliberately left the flute off to leave fans and people like me to discuss this issue fifty years later and think that was really clever and cool!

Of course, it is a great track without the flute and features one of rock's all-time classic guitar solos. The song is out in the ether, in a ubiquitous fashion.

Maybe it is not quite up there with "We Are The Champions", as an iconic rock anthem for example, but "Aqualung" is often the first thing that comes to mind, along with Ian Anderson's signature flute, when people hear the name Jethro Tull.

It may or may not, depending on what you read, have given its name to singer songwriter and contemporary artist Aqualung (who in real life is Matthew Hales). I don't know of any band or artist out there called Locomotive Breath.

"Aqualung" is the opening track of the *Aqualung* album, recorded at Island Studios, London, in January 1971, and released on 19th March 1971. It runs for six minutes and thirty-four seconds.

Due to its length and its mini-symphony episodic structure, it was never released as a single. The lyrics, co-written by Ian Anderson's then-wife Jennie Franks, who had been photographing homeless people for a project, address homelessness and societal attitudes toward it.

The character Aqualung is a homeless tramp who curiously resembles Ian Anderson, as is depicted on the album cover.

The name "Aqualung" refers to the tramp's imagined chesty, rasping, congested breathing, reminiscent of the underwater breathing apparatus. Ian wanted to get a discombobulated telephone voice sound for the early vocals in the song.

To achieve them, all frequencies except those at around 1000 hertz were removed during recording. There is a similar vocal effect on "Song For Jeffrey" from *This Was*.

When it came to recording the guitar solo for "Aqualung," a famous Tull story unfolds: Martin Barre, mid-solo, was unable to wave back to Jimmy Page, who had popped in to say hello.

Inspired by the song and by Jimmy's presence, Martin delivered what *Guitar* magazine later ranked as the 25th best classic rock solo of all time.

Led Zeppelin were recording Led Zeppelin IV in the basement studio at Island during the same period. Remarkably, the solo itself is only one minute and six seconds long.

While "Locomotive Breath" has been played live 1,915 times (as of 22nd December 2023) by Jethro Tull, "Aqualung" has been performed in concert a mere 1,902 times. It is traditionally the first encore song, segueing into "Locomotive Breath".

Over the years, it has sometimes been played with an instrumental introduction featuring echoed flute over a Bo Diddley drum pattern, becoming "Aquadiddley".

Now, I must address the elephant in the room and lay my

cards on the table: I don't like "Aqualung", or at least I don't anymore.

This realisation hit me at a Tull concert in Tunbridge Wells in 2001. To leave the theatre quickly after the encore, I went for my post-gig toilet break early — yes, during the "Aqualung" encore, and I didn't mind.

In the restroom, I met a fellow fan who shared my sentiment. This fan, well known in the Jethro Tull universe (whose identity I won't disclose to protect the guilty), also expressed the same view about the song.

However, we both rushed back for "Locomotive Breath". Can you be a Tull fan and not like "Aqualung"? Can I write this book and not like "Aqualung"?

In the early seventies, I bought the *Aqualung* album on vinyl and loved every song, including the title track. I listened to it hundreds of times and still appreciated it. I recognised it as a great song (which it still is).

But something happened in the nineties. I developed a similar problem with "Stairway To Heaven" by Led Zeppelin.

Both songs are in the upper pantheon of revered and worshipped classic rock, and I don't like either of them anymore. They're overplayed, leaving me bored and disinterested. I can't really say why, though. I still love virtually everything else put out by Tull, especially "Locomotive Breath", which also dates from 1971 and is fifty-two years old.

When "Aqualung" first came out, I would have given it a 9/10. Now, I would rate it only 4/10. However, I need to reconsider before I get into serious trouble! The song has listed status, is part of our rock heritage, and is loved by millions. Even my wife, who is not a Tull fan, likes it. For my own personal safety and integrity, I might just sneak it up to a 7.5/10, or maybe even an 8.

© Bekah Elliott

8.
Locomotive Breath
The one that never slows down

"**L**ocomotive Breath" has been, is, and will continue to be the most popular song ever done by Jethro Tull. I have, at last count, fourteen different versions: one original studio track and thirteen live versions and variations from across the years, played by every different line-up.

I have "Locomotive Breath" on vinyl, tape, CD, VHS video, and DVD. I've played the track at home, in the car, and even in public for friends thousands of times. I've seen Tull and Ian Anderson live fifteen times, and needless to say, it has been the final full track in the encore on every occasion. I have never tired of it!

So just how many times has "Locomotive Breath" been played live? Here are some comparisons to other classic rock tracks up to 22nd December 2023:

"School's Out" by Alice Cooper: 2,874 times

"(Don't Fear) The Reaper" by Blue Öyster Cult: 2,524 times

"Smoke On The Water" by Deep Purple: 2,143 times

"Born To Run" by Bruce Springsteen: 1,802 times

"Your Song" by Elton John: 2,451 times (played at every live concert since its release in 1970)

As for "Locomotive Breath", the breakdown is as follows: Jethro Tull has played it live 1,915 times, Ian Anderson has performed it 659 times, and Martin Barre with his band has played it 214 times, making a total of 2,788 performances from 1971 to 2023.

Ian and Martin, of course, played on the original studio version. In 1971, the year it was released, it was played forty-one times by Jethro Tull, while fifty-two years later, in 2023, it was played ninety times by both Jethro Tull and the Martin Barre Band.

"Locomotive Breath" is not only one of the most played live songs in the rock and pop world, but also one of the most popular live rock songs of all time by any artist.

Not bad for a song that was fraught with difficulties during recording. These issues have become part of Jethro Tull mythology. Ian brought the song to the band, and a recording was made, but Ian was not happy with it. Clive was struggling with the groove, so Ian laid down a bass drum and hi-hat rhythm himself. Meanwhile, Martin was not coping either, so Ian played the "chukka chukka" guitar part on Martin's electric guitar.

All was not lost for Clive and Martin, as Clive was able to embellish over the top of the rhythm with tom-tom patterns, while Martin added brilliant lead lines over the "chukka chukka" guitar.

A solid bass line was played by new member Jeffrey Hammond-Hammond, then Ian smashed it with a great flute solo, and John added a touch of brilliance with the ivories in the outro.

However, something was still missing. Lunch was also missing, so the band took a fifteen-minute break. Legend has it that Ian encouraged (or ordered) John to come up with a suitable intro over lunch, similar to the one he did at the start of the live version of "Dharma For One".

In just fifteen minutes, John produced his famous blues-classical introduction to tag onto the front of "Locomotive Breath". The intro lasts forty-two seconds, while the whole song is four minutes and twenty-six seconds long. The intro is so well-known and iconic that one might wonder if John Evan should have received a writing credit?

Lyrically, the song reflects on a train that won't slow down, serving as a metaphor for rampant exponential population growth (2, 4, 8, 16, 32, etc.) leading to the end of the world as we know it. Quite a cheerful song for a live encore!

Notably, it is the only song I am aware of to mention Gideon's Bible in the lyrics. This small Bible, often found in hotel rooms, would have been seen by Ian while on tour. The lyric "was open at page one" refers to the book of Genesis (not the band), which contains the story of Creation (definitely not the 1960s pre-prog rock band of the same name either) and Adam and Eve.

Over the years, each Tull keyboard player has had to play John Evan's piano licks and embellish it themselves, if possible. In more recent years (well, the last thirty), both Andy Giddings and John O'Hara have had lots of fun playing it.

In the eighties, Eddie Jobson, Peter-John Vitesse, Don Airey, and Martin Allcock all played versions rooted in Evan's original. However, none have ever improved upon John's iconic rendition.

Unsurprisingly for such a toe-tapping song, there have been plenty of covers — at least thirty-three found so far. One of the best is a metalled version by Styx.

The live versions of "Locomotive Breath" are great, although early on they were sometimes played with sloppy enthusiasm. By the 2000s, the live performances were metronomically spot-on. However, I still prefer the original studio version for its "chukka chukka" groove and precision.

As indicated in the previous chapter, whilst I have tired of "Aqualung", the same can't be said for "Locomotive Breath". I can't quite put my finger on why. Could it be that the rhythm and chord sequence are vaguely similar to "The Jean Genie" by David Bowie and "Blockbuster" by Sweet? Now there's a thought! It still gets a 9/10 from me.

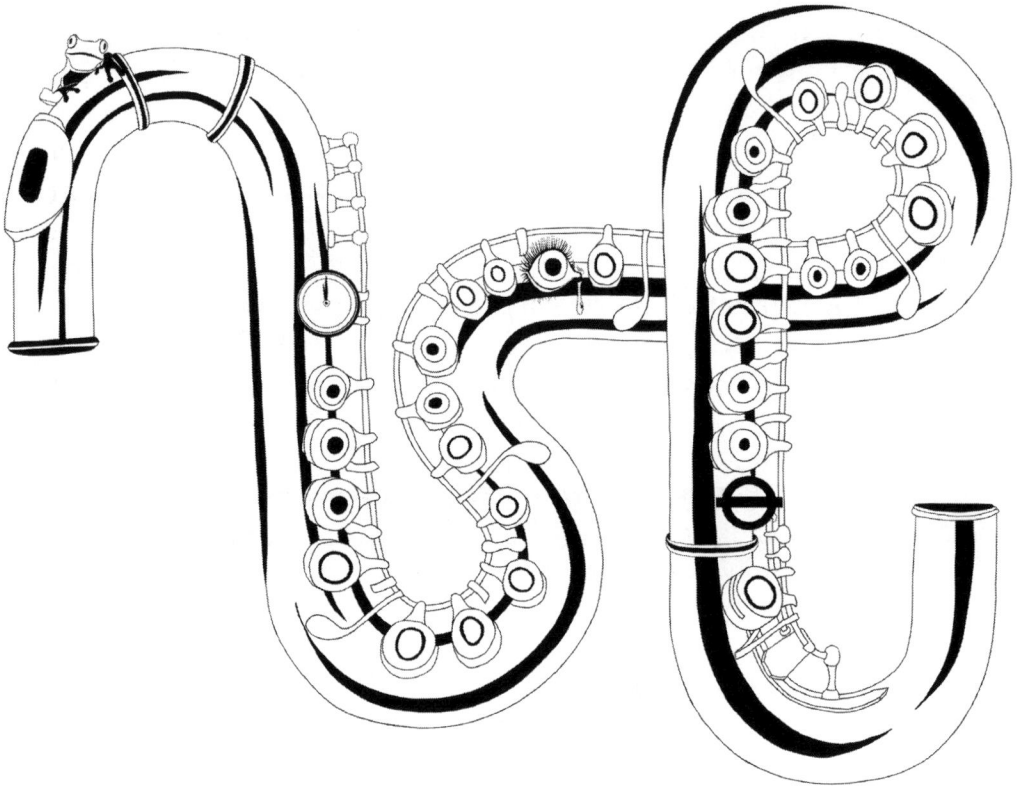

9.
Life Is A Long Song
And in the beginning

April 2020 was a worrying time for everyone, as COVID-19 took off and we were mainly confined to our homes in lockdown. My brother-in-law Andrew and his teenage son Jeremy decided to give a musical concert over Zoom one lunchtime for family and friends, playing a mix of classical, rock, and pop.

Andrew, a professional violinist, had played live and in studios for orchestras for many years. At the time, he was mainly working as a music teacher, with musical preferences predominantly classical, although he was partial to a bit of Frank Zappa occasionally. Jeremy, gifted on all types of guitars, had confidently assured me there was nothing he couldn't play, and I believed him.

When Andrew announced the next song was for his brother-in-law Richard, I was absolutely delighted when they performed "Life Is A Long Song".

Jeremy picked out the single lines and chords on the acoustic guitar like an old pro, while Andrew made the singing and flute lines soar with his violin.

It was a little moment during COVID that really cheered me up and was a great gesture. I messaged Andrew immediately to thank him and Jeremy. It was a great version that didn't even need the one-legged flute player to join in.

I briefly mentioned this song in the introduction, and I still hold the same sentiment — I love it. Released in September 1971 as part of an EP, an "extended player" single, side one featured

"Life Is A Long Song" and "Up The Pool".

The latter is a nostalgic nod to Blackpool, mentioning "my mum's jam sarnies and to see our Auntie Flo". It has always puzzled me how Americans could relate to Tull's English colloquialisms at the time.

Side two included "Dr. Bogenbroom", one of Ian's most cheerful songs about death, followed by "For Later", an instrumental, and "Nursie", a solo acoustic song dedicated to angelic nurses everywhere.

All were great tracks. I acquired the EP on loan in 1972, never returned it, and unbelievably, I still have my "Twist And Shout" Beatles EP from 1963.

Sadly, I don't have a record player anymore, and the EP is tucked away in the loft, which often seems to be the graveyard for a lot of old men's vinyl collections.

The ensemble playing was brilliant throughout, driven by the new drummer Barrie Barlow. He must have felt like he'd hit rock 'n' roll heaven in joining Jethro Tull. His stint in the band lasted nine years, during which Ian christened him Barriemore as his stage name.

Lyrically, "Life Is A Long Song" reflects Ian Anderson's characteristic blend of optimism and pessimism. While the title suggests optimism, the final line, "but the tune ends too soon for us all", introduces a note of pessimism. This dichotomy is typical of Anderson's songwriting style. It's worth noting that around this time, Ian's father was ill, which may have influenced the tone of his lyrics in this song and "Dr. Bogenbroom."

I am also fond of the rendition of "Life Is A Long Song" featured on the *Living With The Past* live CD/DVD from 2001.

In this version, Ian is accompanied by a live string quartet comprising Brian Thomas and Justine Tomlinson on violins, Malcolm Henderson on viola, and Juliet Tomlinson on cello. They provide backing for Ian, Andy Giddings on piano, and Ian's son, James Duncan, on drums.

For me, "Life Is A Long Song" is unquestionably a top ten song, despite its modest peak at number 11 on the UK singles chart. It holds a perfect 10/10 rating in my book. Ending on a note of optimism, life remains a long song, even though "the tune ends too soon for us all". It's a timeless Tull classic that could easily claim the top spot among all-time favourite Tull songs.

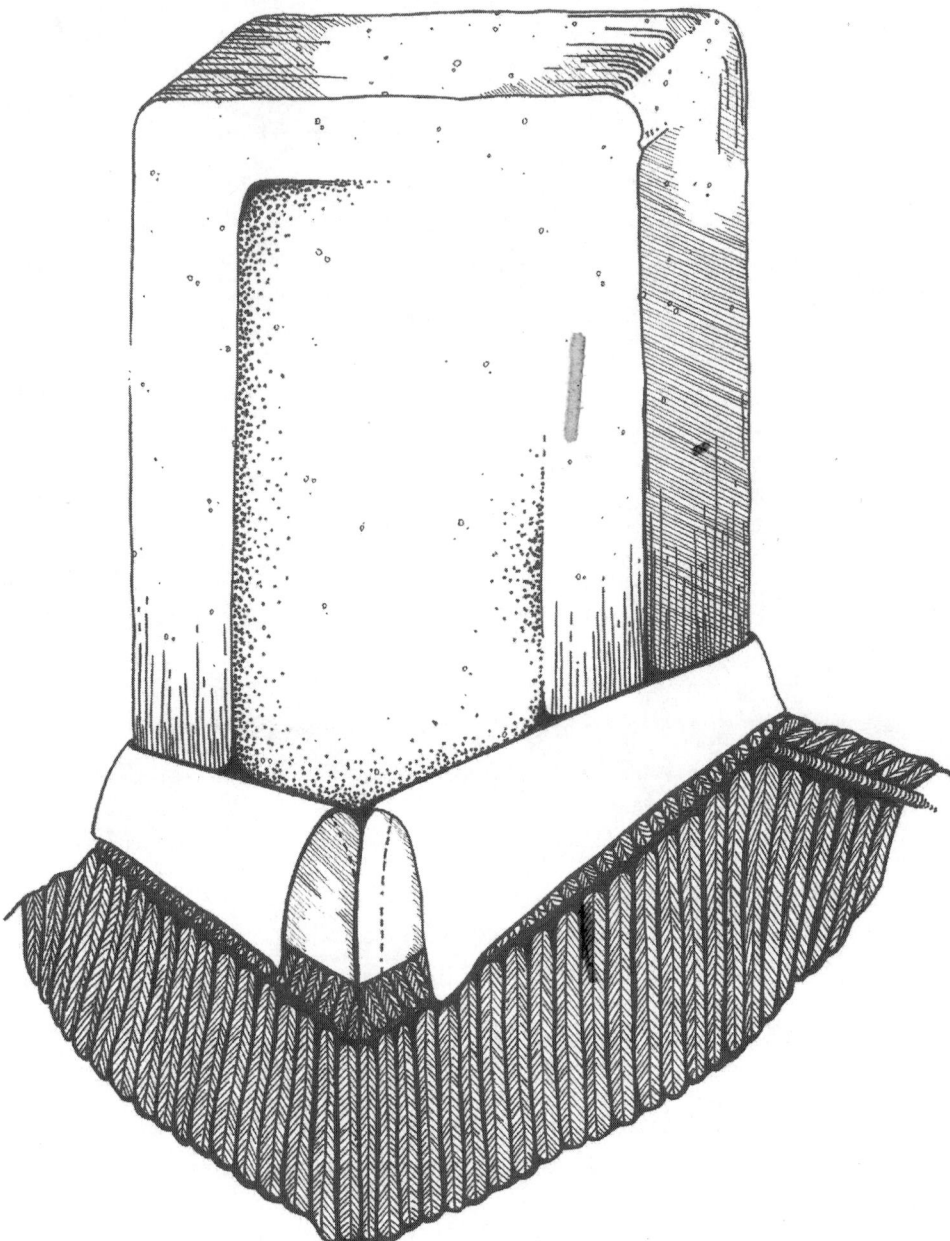

10.
Thick As A Brick
Hello Gerald Bostock

"Thick As A Brick," has been treated as one continuous song for most of its existence. Although the 40th Anniversary Edition in 2012 split the song into eight separate parts, I'll continue to regard "Thick As A Brick" as a single, uninterrupted piece for the sake of this book and chapter.

Originally conceived during the early seventies' era of the concept album, the decision to make it a seamless track was intentional, as longer songs were favoured at the time.

During the initial tours following its release, Jethro Tull performed it in its entirety, and Ian Anderson continued this tradition during his 2012-13 tours featuring both "Thick As A Brick" (1) and "Thick As A Brick (2)", released as an album in 2012. That's a solid forty-three minutes of continuous music without so much as a break for a toilet trip.

The recording of "Thick As A Brick" is steeped in Jethro Tull folklore, with moments ranging from surreal to special to downright silly, all contributing to the unique essence of the album.

While it might seem tempting to craft a single, forty-three-minute paragraph filled with existential musings, pearls of wisdom, and clichés to encapsulate "Thick As A Brick", I'll refrain from that endeavour to spare us all.

The music itself is a complex yet captivating tapestry, offering layers of intricacy and challenge while still inviting listeners to sing along, play air flute, and tap their feet. It's a sublime masterpiece that manages to maintain an accessible touch, ensuring that both the common man (me) and woman can find something to relate to within its depths.

The recording process for "Thick As A Brick" spanned two weeks, followed by an additional two weeks for overdubbing. Ian brought in song fragments, which the band then developed into cohesive pieces.

Barrie Barlow, the new drummer (dubbed Barriemore by Ian for publicity), contributed significantly to the music. David (now Dee) Palmer provided string arrangements, while additional instruments like sax and violin by Ian, harpsichord by John, lute by Martin, and timpani by Barrie were incorporated into the mix.

Ian had already drafted some lyrics, with help of a precocious eight-year-old genius called Gerald Bostock, who contributed greatly. He was old beyond his years, with his writing of mature, profound and surreal concepts about the human condition woven in.

It seemed he had been around the block a bit for someone so young. However, perhaps this was intentional — a playful nod from Ian and Gerald to the album's overarching concept.

"Thick As A Brick" was conceived as a substantial concept album, with a subtle touch of ironic self-awareness that left room for interpretation.

Ian has famously always claimed that "Thick As A Brick" is a bit of a mickey-take; a send-up of its contemporaries who were too overblown and too serious.

The brilliance of Ian and Gerald lay in their ability to allow the album to be interpreted in multiple ways — both as a sincere exploration of profound themes and as a tongue-in-cheek parody.

So, listeners and readers, the question remains: is it serious or satire? The answer is yours to decide.

The album cover was quite the endeavour. Crafted by Ian, Jeffrey, and John, they collaborated with assistance from the record company, Chrysalis, to create a twelve-page provincial newspaper.

Within its pages, the child prodigy Gerald Bostock contributed his epic poem "Thick As A Brick", which graced the centrefold. Surprisingly, the production of the newspaper cover took even longer than that of the album itself.

Recorded in December 1971 and released in March 1972, "Thick As A Brick" achieved impressive chart success, reaching number 5 in the UK album chart and claiming the top spot in the USA — an astonishing feat given its distinctly English flavour.

Lyrics like "good old Ernie, he coughed up a tenner on a Premium Bond win", would surely bamboozle most Americans. To help, a translation would go like this: "The UK national savings computer nicknamed Ernie gave out a £10 bank note on the premium bond national lottery".

Despite any linguistic hurdles, American fans embraced the music, unfazed by the fact that most of the lyrics were penned by an eight-year-old. This continued a trend of American enthusiasm for British music, established since the heyday of The Beatles.

While contemporary critics offered mixed reviews, "Thick As A Brick" has since been recognised as a seminal work that profoundly influenced numerous musicians.

Icons like Steve Harris of Iron Maiden, Geddy Lee of Rush, and Joe Bonamassa have hailed it as a "true master class" in music. In subsequent years, it consistently ranks in the top ten of prog rock albums in various polls.

Its enduring impact led to the creation of "Thick As A Brick (2)" in 2012, continuing the story of Gerald Bostock, now forty-eight years old, who had experienced a series of ups and downs in life. Gerald's collaboration with Ian also extended to the writing of Ian's solo album Homo Erraticus in 2014.

As mentioned earlier, both Jethro Tull and Ian Anderson have performed the entire piece live. Occasionally, they would play excerpts, often including sections like "Really Don't Mind" and "The Upper Class" from side one of the vinyl.

During performances, there were instances where a telephone would ring, interrupting the piece. Ian would play along and answer it, although there was a rumour that this was Gerald Bostock trying to wind Ian up, which Gerald denies.

"Thick As A Brick" holds the distinction of being the first forty-minute continuous piece of music with proper vocals released in the rock genre at the time. Comparatively, other lengthy compositions from the era included Yes' "Close To The

Edge" (on the album of the same name (1972)), which clocked in at just under nineteen minutes on one side, and Genesis' "Supper's Ready", spanning twenty-three minutes on their *Foxtrot* album (1972).

Emerson Lake and Palmer's "Karn Evil 9" from *Brain Salad Surgery* (1973) reached over twenty-nine minutes but was still considerably shorter than "Thick As A Brick".

Released shortly after "Thick As A Brick", Mike Oldfield's *Tubular Bells* (1973) ran for forty-nine minutes and eighteen seconds, although it lacked meaningful lyrics, featuring only endearing but unintelligible vocalisations Mike put on side two.

While there's no exact specification for what a concept album should be, compositions with one overarching theme or song exceeding twenty or forty minutes, conveying deep and meaningful music and lyrics, certainly fit the bill.

All a little bit pretentious? It did not worry Ian. Jethro Tull were to do it all again with *A Passion Play* the following year!

I'd rate "Thick As A Brick" a solid 9.5 out of 10. While side two of the vinyl meanders a bit too much for my taste, it still earns a respectable 9. Side one, on the other hand, is sheer perfection, deserving of a resounding 10 for its conceptual brilliance.

I am indebted to Gerald Bostock for advice and insight about "Thick As A Brick", and for proofreading.

11.
The Story Of The Hare Who Lost His Spectacles
Always leave a spare pair of glasses with someone you can trust

After recording *Thick As A Brick* and touring the album, Jethro Tull decided to go the full monty and produce the mother of all concept albums. This time, there could be no irony, and no having it both ways: this one was to be suitably serious, deep, and meaningful.

It would be a play on the human condition, especially after death, which could prove to be a bit tricky! This is the story of "A Passion Play" and the man (Ronnie Pilgrim) who lost his life, and what happened subsequently to his soul. The album is not exactly a bundle of laughs, and some levity and light relief was perhaps needed midway through.

In medieval times when passion plays were performed, they would be often interrupted by a comic interlude. Whilst the play itself would be serious and deeply religious, the interlude would be fun, often pagan, deliberately bawdy, and with no connection whatsoever to the main Passion Play story. After the comic break, the serious business of the The Passion Play would resume.

This was the approach adopted by Tull halfway through

their "Passion Play" (now hence referred to as "The Play"). Side one of "The Play" on vinyl lasts twenty-two minutes and thirty-nine seconds, followed by the first one minute and thirty seconds of "The Story Of The Hare Who Lost His Spectacles" (henceforth referred to as "The Story").

Turning over the vinyl, you get another two minutes and forty-eight seconds of "The Story" and another nineteen minutes and ten seconds of "The Play". This means that just nine and a half percent of the whole "A Passion Play" consists of "The Story".

While most reviewers and fans welcomed the addition of "The Story", many did not like having to turn over the vinyl record partway through.

Some fans and critics thought "The Play" might have been better without "The Story". However, this is not my view. At least the vinyl turnover gave some disgruntled fans a halftime break with tea and cake to mull over what they had heard so far.

Musically, "The Story" is impeccable, composed of piano, glockenspiel, and wind instruments written by John and Ian, with additional string orchestration by David Palmer. It perfectly supports the narrative to come. John introduces the story with a vocal flourish, while Jeffrey speaks the words in an exaggerated, tongue-rolling Lancashire accent, adding a unique charm.

There has been extensive analysis on the Internet and elsewhere about the meaning of the lyrics in "The Play" and "The Story".

I will not delve into those interpretations here because I don't always follow them. Much like time signatures, I don't always get lyrics. However, why not take the lyrics at face value? My own conclusion is that Jeffrey's words are simply good fun. They read well, they scan well, and they tell a cute, Alice In Wonderland-type fable about a hare who has lost his spectacles and is helped by his friends to find them.

In the end, it all works out because he has a "spare pair". While it's not much of a punch line, it resonates with me as someone who frequently misplaces their glasses and needs a spare pair in reserve. It could just be a whimsical tale about the everyday struggles of the visually restricted.

For the "Passion Play" tours, the decision was made to

create a film for "The Story" to replace a live performance. This seven-minute film, which can easily be found on the Internet, allowed the band to take a break for tea, a cigarette, or a quick restroom visit (though not for illicit drugs!).

Unlike "Thick As A Brick" live performances, this interval provided a brief respite. The film, a grand little production, cost £12,000 (about $30,000). I am sure Tull recouped the expenses from the subsequent sold-out tours.

The critical reaction to "The Play" in general, and to "The Story" specifically, was, to put it politely, very mixed. In fact, most reviewers thought it was awful.

Some fans love "The Play" but hate "The Story", and vice versa, while others dislike both but enjoy the rest of Tull's work.

Ian is now quite damning in his comments about "The Play", though he shouldn't be, as it is still a great album — certainly above average in Jethro Tull's body of work. Jeffrey remains wryly amused by "The Story", and I suspect that if he had his time again, he would do it completely differently... up to a point.

Perhaps "The Story Of The Hare Who Lost His Mind"? However, he would be unlikely to have a spare pair of "brains". With that, I will take my own tea break and then have a lie down.

I am fond of *A Passion Play* and would give it 7/10. However, strange man that I am, I like "The Story Of The Hare Who Lost His Spectacles" even more. It is totally unlike anything else in the Tull catalogue, and it wasn't all down to Ian Anderson.

The fact that Jeffrey got to shine, supported by John, is very good. For example, if you compare it with the heavy metal approach of "Steel Monkey" from the 1987 *Crest Of A Knave* album, you would never think in a million years that both tracks could be by the same band.

The casual absurdity, Monty Pythonesque humour, and the almost deliberately weak, non-punchy punch line all appeal to me, along with the great music.

It is also exactly the right length — a full album of "The Story" might push the joke too far. I will give it 8/10 for the split vinyl versions and 8.5/10 for the continuous CD version.

12.
Skating Away On The Thin Ice Of The New Day
Meanwhile, back in the year 1974

This next song features a title with thirty-four letters, twelve syllables, and ten words, making it the second-longest titled Tull track.

I think you might be able to guess the first; the clue is "animal glasses". This song was supposedly about global cooling, a popular topic in the 1970s. It also marks the first use of a piano accordion by John Evan in Tull's history.

The accordion is featured throughout the *War Child* album on songs like "Queen And Country" and, more specifically, "Skating Away on the Thin Ice of the New Day" (henceforth known as "Skating").

The piano accordion is widely used globally in folk and traditional music, from the Tango in Argentina to Cajun and Zydeco music in the Americas, and to Celtic and Scottish Ceilidh music closer to home.

It was rarely used in pop and rock music in the sixties, seventies, and eighties, probably because it was "fiendishly difficult to play", as Ian Anderson has pointed out in live concerts over the years.

Some musicologists agree it is difficult to play, while others argue that if you can play the piano and co-ordinate both hands, it is easy. Starting with John Evan, every Tull keyboard player has mastered it over the years, especially Andy Giddings, whom I saw play it live many times in the 1990s. Giddings managed to look cool and upstanding, not seated stage left and hidden behind his keyboards.

The piano accordion was particularly well-used during live renditions of "Fat Man" from the *Stand Up* album, even though it wasn't used in the studio version.

As it has bellows that are squeezed to produce notes by air, it can sound a little like an organ. Despite its perceived difficulty, it appears on a surprising number of songs from this era.

According to *Pop Matters*, which highlighted forty-one piano accordion songs including "Skating", the most famous piano accordion song is "Squeeze Box" by The Who, which became an unexpected hit in 1975.

Pete Townshend claimed to have written it as a joke and learned to play the instrument in an afternoon. Another notable use is the live version of "Tusk" by Fleetwood Mac, where Christine McVie used the piano accordion to replicate the entire marching band that played on the studio recording.

Other instrumentation includes the wonderful glockenspiel, played by the musical drummer Barrie, as well as the more conventional guitar, mandolin, flute, bass, and drums.

The melody, which I just love, is Celtic, folksy, flowing, and uplifting. Adding a driving bass after the "rabbit on the run" lyric at 2:45 is a masterstroke. Again, it's sing-along time, with spontaneous foot tapping.

"Meanwhile back in the year one": I do find the lyrics a tad perplexing. Ian says the lyrics are about global cooling. This was a 1970s idea that the use of aerosols and a variation in the tilt of the Earth (orbital forcing) would lead to a cooling of global temperatures. As we now know, and as Ian has pointed out, the lyrics to this song are now redundant, as exactly the opposite is happening with global warming.

However, others, needless to say, have their own view of the lyrics. There is a reference to *A Passion Play* in the lyrics; "Skating" was first written in mid-1973 after the release of *A Passion Play*, and there are lyrics about "the universal minds writing you into the passion play".

So, is this more God referencing coming from Ian then? But what does that have to do with global cooling? Other fan lyrical interpretations include opinions on "life after death", "a new start", and "seize the day".

As per usual, as throughout this book, I just do not quite get the meaning, but then do others? That is if there is one to be had, of course. However, as I've said before, I do enjoy that Ian's lyrics are just out of reach of my full understanding.

I like the air of some mystery. Do you always have to fully understand the lyrics to enjoy a song? Anyway, that is my excuse for perhaps being a little "Thick As A Brick".

"Skating" kicks off side two of the vinyl edition of *War Child* and clocks in at four minutes and nine seconds. Written in 1972, it was formally recorded on 19th December 1973, and released as part of the *War Child* album on 14th October 1974.

While it was released as a single in early 1975 and only reached number 75 in the USA, it was universally praised by critics, even though the *War Child* album as a whole received mixed reviews.

Among fans, it regularly polls among the top ten Tull songs. Over the years, it has been played live on an intermittent basis.

I rather like the song, even if I don't quite get the lyrics. It would be a Tull 7/10 from me, but I'll give it a sneaky 8/10 for the use of the piano accordion.

13.
Baker St Muse
It's a no-show from
Sherlock Holmes and Gerry Rafferty

Baker Street, named after London builder William Baker, is a well-known thoroughfare in Marylebone, central north London. Running north to south, it is famously the fictional home of detective Sherlock Holmes at 221b Baker Street. Historically, the area comprised residential flats in the 1970s, but had transitioned to mainly commercial properties by the 2020s.

Baker Street is also renowned for featuring the most famous saxophone motif/solo in rock and pop music. The song "Baker Street" by Gerry Rafferty, released in 1978, is a four-minute pop classic highlighted by an alto sax solo by session player Raphael Ravenscroft.

This song reached number 3 in the UK charts and number 2 in the USA. Despite sharing a name, there is no musical or stylistic connection between the 1978 "Baker Street" and Jethro Tull's 1975 "Baker St. Muse."

So, what about "Baker St. Muse", the second most famous song written about this thoroughfare? It was composed around December 1974 or January 1975, with some help from David Palmer. The song was recorded on 15th May 1975, and released as part of the *Minstrel In The Gallery* album in early September 1975. It lasts sixteen minutes and thirty-nine seconds, divided into four parts.

In January 1975, workaholic Ian travelled alone to Los

71

Angeles to continue writing the *Minstrel In The Gallery* album. David Palmer joined him to integrate string arrangements into the songs — not just for embellishment, but as an integral part of the tracks. Recording then took place in Monaco using the Maison Rouge Mobile Studio in May 1975.

According to Jethro Tull folklore, this was not a happy time for the band. Ian felt the others were not committed enough, what with them being distracted by the sights of the Principality and dealing with personal issues.

Consequently, Ian worked on arrangements for the entire album on his own, only bringing in the full band at a later point.

Musically, "Baker St. Muse" is just amazing to me. Ian Anderson's acoustic guitar work in the mid-1970s was at its zenith, influenced by folk artist Roy Harper.

Ian employed single-note playing to transition between chords and often used a capo to raise the key to suit his baritone singing voice. I won't delve further into guitar science, but his playing sounded lucid, flowing, and virtuosic to me, fitting the songs perfectly.

It's quite sad that Ian has lost interest in the acoustic guitar and rarely plays it in 2024, as he was and still is a formidable guitarist. Even if "Baker St. Muse" starts with a joke guitar mistake and has to be redone, his talent shines through.

Martin, John, Jeffrey, Barrie, and Ian as flautist play with their usual skill on "Baker St. Muse", but the other star performer is David Palmer for his string arrangements.

Palmer utilised members of the London Philomusica, including leader Patrick Halling, Elizabeth Edwards, Rita Eddowes, and Bridget Proctor on violins, with Katherine Thulborn on cello. These musicians had also played live with Tull on the War Child tours.

David Palmer, a classically trained musician from the Royal Academy of Music, had been intermittently organising orchestral instrumentation for Tull over the years.

By the time of the *War Child* and *Minstrel In The Gallery* albums, he was more or less a full-time member of Tull, handling arranging duties.

By the end of 1975, he officially joined the band as the second keyboard player and arranger, a role he held until 1980.

His compositional contributions to Tull's late seventies folk trilogy albums cannot be overstated, and his string arrangement on "Baker St. Muse" is particularly noteworthy.

After his time with Tull, Palmer continued with orchestral and arranging work. Following the death of his wife Margaret in 1998, he transitioned and became Dee Palmer.

Dee has played a significant role in the Jethro Tull story, much like George Martin did for The Beatles, whose producing and arranging skills were instrumental in shaping their sound.

Then there were the lyrics. Wow, what brilliant words, and I think I actually understand most of them most of the time in "Baker St. Muse". By the mid-seventies, Ian was living in a flat on Baker Street near the Marylebone Road, observing all of life from his window and down on the street. The lyrics are seedy, profound, vulgar, compassionate, self-reflective, and melancholic (and that's all in the first stanza).

"Baker St. Muse" begins with the observer walking down Baker Street, noting the seedier sides of life while pursuing a girl for some romantic interest (I think).

A musical interlude, "Nice Little Tune", leads into "Pig-Me And The Whore", where Ian Anderson really goes for the sexual jugular. Overflowing with erupting sexual innuendo, this might be the most amazing Tull lyrics ever — crude yet wonderfully entertaining (and definitely not something that would be written today).

This leads us then "into the Marylebone Road" for "Crash-Barrier Waltzer". Here, in stark contrast, the lyrics are sad, poignant, and melancholic, full of compassion for a homeless, struggling old lady.

In "Mother England Reverie", Ian reflects on his own status as a rock star. It starts off sad but turns positive with the line "one day I'll be a minstrel in the gallery", and the music sounds joyous as Ian takes back control.

As Tull accelerates towards the end of the song, I wonder whether Ian got the girl in the end. In 1976, he did marry his second wife, Shona, so it probably did work out.

Even more amusingly, he seems to get locked in the studio at the end ("I can't get out!"). That was a nice joke after the heavy-duty lyrics in "Baker St. Muse". Luckily, he was out in time to complete "Grace" — the last song on the album.

The song has generally been well received by critics, especially for the wonderful contrasting lyrics. However, despite extensive research, rumour has it the track was never actually played live, certainly not in full.

There was a 1982 song by Sparks called "Sherlock Holmes", which definitely ranks third among tracks related to Baker Street and scores a bemusing 5/10.

The big one, "Baker Street" by Gerry Rafferty, is a perfect pop song and earns a 7/10. "Baker St Muse", as classic mid-seventies Jethro Tull, gets an 8/10 for great music, but the lyrics, courtesy of the genius of Ian Anderson, deserve a 10/10. It all averages out to 10/10 overall. Maths was never my strong point.

14.
Too Old To Rock 'n' Roll:
Too Young To Die!
Going on 80 is the new 30

As of January 2024, the combined ages of Mick Jagger, Keith Richards, and Ronnie Wood from The Rolling Stones total two hundred and sixteen years.

Bruce Springsteen is a comparatively young seventy-four, while from the Jethro Tull family, Ian Anderson is seventy-six and Martin Barre is seventy-seven. All of these musicians continue to tour and record. Paul McCartney, at eighty-one, plays bass, guitar, and piano, still remembering the lyrics to all those classic Beatles songs. Elton John, now seventy-six, has supposedly retired from touring, but as a sit-down piano player, any potential comeback / farewell tour should be easy for him.

It seems you're never "too old to rock 'n' roll", as Ian Anderson aptly coined the phrase in 1975 when he was just twenty-eight.

Any age is, of course, "too young to die". This can be taken literally or as a metaphor for the potential demise of a rock star's career as musical tastes evolve. It appears that being over eighty in rock and roll is the new sixty, which was the new forty, which, in turn, was the new twenty-eight.

In 1975, no one, least of all Ian Anderson, had any idea how long a rock and roll career or a rock and roll life would last.

And so, one of the great cliché-titled rock songs was born: "Too Old To Rock 'n' Roll: Too Young To Die". Both album and song had the same title, so forever, or at least to the end of this chapter, each will be known respectively as Too Old (A) and "Too Old" (S).

The album was conceived as a stage play, which never got off the ground. It was about an ageing rocker, Ray Lomas, who gets overtaken by modernity and refuses to update. He then dies in a motorbike accident, only to be resurrected to find that he, the ageing rocker, has come back into fashion.

Ian Anderson insists it was not autobiographical but rather about other late-twenty-something ageing rock stars around in 1975. This year saw the start of punk, and bands like Pink Floyd, Genesis, Yes, and Jethro Tull came to be seen as rock dinosaurs. Yet, only a few years later, all four bands were back in fashion and selling zillions of albums. Jethro Tull, with their late-seventies folk rock trilogy of albums, would be as big as ever.

"Too Old" (S) was written in December 1975 and then subsequently recorded with the Maison Rouge Mobile in Brussels. As with "Baker St Muse", Ian had some compositional help from David Palmer. It was put out as a single in March 1976 and as part of "Too Old" (A) on the 23rd April 1976.

Instrumentally, the album was a full band effort with additional orchestration by David Palmer. It also featured backing vocals from Maddy Prior of Steeleye Span and new bass player John Glascock.

John, a fluid and melodic bass player influenced by Paul McCartney, had come from a flamenco prog rock band called Carmen that had toured with Tull. When Jeffrey announced he was leaving Tull to return to painting in 1975, Ian remembered John. Being a more natural musician than Jeffrey, John needed less help in working out bass lines.

"Too Old" (S) tells the story of an old rocker who has an accident and perishes. Although the lyrics are sad, the joyous chorus hints at recovery and redemption for Ray, the protagonist.

This is confirmed in the next song, "Pied Piper", where Ray is resurrected. Ian says the title came to him during a difficult plane journey, where excessive turbulence caused the line "too old to rock n roll: too young to die" to pop into his head. It would have been a suitably ironic line for a headstone if the plane had crashed!

It has always amazed me that in the 1970s, being twenty-eight years old and approaching thirty was considered "past it" in a rock 'n' roll sense.

Bands and fans alike could not conceive that fifty years later, they would still be recording and touring. With Jethro Tull, The Rolling Stones, or even Willie Nelson still performing at ninety, as Van Morrison said, "It is too late to stop now".

"Too Old" (S) has been played live on and off over the years. In the late seventies, musical polymath David Palmer played a sax solo towards the end of the song. The critics and fans alike (including me) did not really like Too Old (A), but "Too Old" (S) received nothing but praise. It still makes some top ten Tull song lists.

I did not like the album, but am fond of the song – although it might not make my particular Tull top ten. I like the lyrics as a story.

If you compare and contrast them with other Tull lyrics that are obtuse, deep, and out-of-reach, then "Too Old" (S) is very accessible and relatable. It is also the only song I know that has "spark plugs" in the lyrics, so for that alone, I will give it a Strictly Come Tull 7/10.

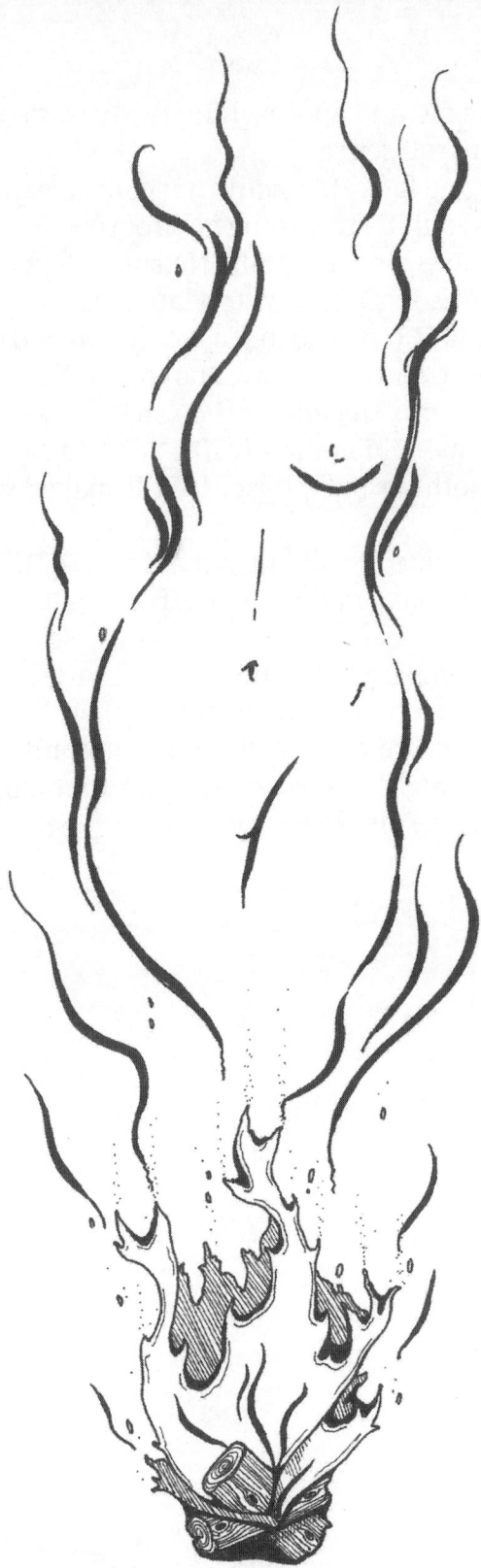

© Bekah Elliott

15.
Fire At Midnight
Keep the home fire burning

In 1973, Dave Gilmour sang "Home, home again, I like to be here when I can. When I come home cold and tired, it's good to warm my bones beside the fire".

With lyrics written by Roger Waters, this is the second to last verse of "Time" from *The Dark Side Of The Moon* album.

To me, it captures the longing for the comforts of home, that emotional warmth, and the sense of belonging after a challenging day on tour.

Alongside the iconic line, "Hanging on in quiet desperation is the English way" from earlier in "Time", these lyrics resonate deeply with me, and the musical track isn't too bad either.

Three and bit years later, some more lyrics came to my attention: "Kindled by the dying embers of another working day, go upstairs take off your make up, fold your clothes neatly away. Me, I'll sit and write this love song, as I all too seldom do. Build a little fire at midnight, it's good to be back home with you."

Those words were written and sung by Ian Anderson on "Fire At Midnight", which features on *Songs From The Wood* released in early 1977.

Just like the lyrics in "Time", to me, the ones on "Fire At Midnight" feel reminiscent of the longing for domestic comforts, the emotional warmth and sense of belonging that only a home can provide after a hard day of touring.

It's the same again! This time though, the singer was inspired to write a rare love song "as I all too seldom do", rather than just "warm [his] bones beside the fire".

Two distinct songs, two different bands, yet I've been mentally linking these songs together through their lyrics for years — call me a mad, sad fool if you will.

The more detailed "Time" analysis will have to wait for my book, Waters Verses Gilmour: A Mad, Sad Compendium of Pink Floyd in 3 and ½ Court Cases (or Albums). I jest, but meanwhile, let's get back to "Fire At Midnight".

In 1976, Ian married Shona, his wife to this day, and they moved to a farm estate in Buckinghamshire, finally settling into a proper family home with the anticipation of children on the horizon.

Up until then, Ian had lived a nomadic lifestyle, constantly on the move. As a token of appreciation for the rural escape they now enjoyed, Ian received a book titled "Folklore, Myths and Legends of Britain", authored by Russell Ash and published in 1973.

This book had a profound impact on *Songs From The Wood*, influencing both its music and lyrics. The album uniquely blended medieval minstrel, folk, and traditional musical elements with loud, bombastic rock, a fusion rarely replicated since.

This influence extended to *Heavy Horses* and *Stormwatch*, the other two albums in the folk-rock trilogy.

Lyrically, *Songs From The Wood* evoked a rural idyll, with songs like "Jack In The Green" exploring the mythical Green Man and "Velvet Green", which subtly intertwined mythical themes with sensuality. "Fire At Midnight," however, stood out as a simple love song, expressing a yearning for the comforts of home.

Following strained relations within the band during the making of *Minstrel In The Gallery* and *Too Old To Rock 'n' Roll: Too Young To Die*, a sense of harmony and camaraderie prevailed during the creation of *Songs From The Wood*.

All band members contributed to the arrangements, with Ian often stepping aside at Morgan Studios to allow them space to develop musical ideas. David Palmer, now a full-time band member, and Martin played significant roles in this collaborative effort. The ensemble performance on "Fire At

Midnight" particularly stands out to me as being truly brilliant.

The song's structure is straightforward: verse one, followed by verse two, then an instrumental break, and finally a repeat of verse two, all within about two minutes and thirty seconds.

Both Ian's and my favourite part seems to be verse two, which is repeated twice. During the instrumental break, a blend of acoustic and electric guitars, mandolin, and piano creates a delightful weave of melodies.

A second recorded version appears on *The Jethro Tull Christmas Album* (2003), which is similar but features a more prominent flute in the instrumental break and a grander sound with swelling organs.

Generally, it's believed that version one is superior, as it feels more cohesive, rather than merely assembled from its separate parts.

It's worth noting that "Fire At Midnight" should not be mistaken for "Fires At Midnight" by Blackmore's Night, a considerably longer track released in 2001. While both are folk rock, with Ritchie Blackmore, a devoted Tull fan, delivering a spirited guitar solo, the latter is not a cover version of the former.

For a bit of fun, I'll give "Time" by Pink Floyd an 8/10 for its poignant lyrics about home. Likewise, "Fires At Midnight" by Blackmore's Night earns a playful 7/10. But when it comes to Jethro Tull, the rating remains a steadfast and resounding 10/10 for "Fire At Midnight": no ifs, ands, or buts.

Rock 'n' Roll

16.
Pibroch (Cap In Hand)
Bagpipes and rock'n'roll

Bagpipes feature a bag known as the chanter, serving as a kind of bellows from which air is squeezed out. As the air escapes slowly, it passes over various reeds, resulting in an almost single-tone clarinet-like sound.

When these reed sounds combine, they produce the distinctive traditional bagpipe sound. Beneath this, there's often a single, continuous lower tone, aptly named the drone, which persists throughout the performance.

This instrument is purely acoustic and doesn't require any electrical amplification, making it quite un-rock 'n' roll. Additionally, variations of this instrument exist worldwide, often in the form of a bellows-driven wind instrument. Our focus, however, is on the Scottish subspecies.

Paul McCartney incorporated bagpipes from The Cambletown Pipe Band into the ending of "Mull Of Kintyre", a move that contributed to its success as a chart-topping single for nine weeks in 1979.

Bagpipes are seldom used in rock or pop music, but there are a few notable exceptions. Roy Wood played bagpipes on the Wizard hit "Are You Ready To Rock" in 1974, fitting into his trend of exploring various musical instruments.

Scottish-born AC/DC singer Bon Scott surprised many by playing bagpipes on "It's A Long Way To The Top (If You Wanna Rock 'n' Roll)" in 1975, creating an unexpected fusion. However, imagine the potential impact if AC/DC had stuck with bagpipes instead of guitars!

The Red Hot Chilli Pipers, formed in 2002, deserve a mention for their efforts to blend bagpipes and rock. Their "bagrock" rendition of "Smoke On The Water" is worth a listen, especially if you're in need of something to cheer you up (but perhaps not if you have a headache).

Despite doing extensive research, I couldn't find any evidence of bagpipes being used on a Jethro Tull album. The closest instance is towards the end of the instrumental "Warm Sporran" from *Stormwatch*.

In this piece, "bagpipes" (presumably played by David Palmer on the portative organ) accompany voices, acoustic guitar, mandolin, and flute.

However, Ian did write a song that, if taken literally, would have required an epic bagpipe workout, possibly lasting several hours. Fortunately, Tull's track clocks in at a manageable eight minutes and thirty-three seconds.

"Pibroch" is a Gaelic term referring to a composition for bagpipes. It is characterised by a slow melodic theme played over the continuous drone to create a trance-like effect.

Sans bagpipes, Jethro Tull took this concept, added lyrics, and gave it a rock twist in their song "Pibroch (Cap In Hand)". Why did they do it? Simply because they could. After all, they're Jethro Tull, known for their willingness to take risks and defy convention.

The track kicks off with Martin's cascading guitar licks, echoing in reverse, which some say resemble bagpipes. To me, they're more reminiscent of whale song or an overloaded *Hoover* — but they sound fantastic regardless!

The entire band joins in with crashing intensity until it gradually quiets down for the start of verse one around 1:20 in.

Another minute passes before verse two begins. At 3:23, there's a delightful melodic interlude with the whole band chiming in with a "duh de duh" refrain.

Around 4:15, the intensity picks up again, leading to a folksy jig-like section featuring mandolin, whistle, flute, and handclaps — easily my favourite part of the track.

Then comes some lovely classical noodling, segueing into verse three at 6:50. The track concludes with more epic guitar wailing until it reaches its finish at 8:33.

The lyrics of the song may not be as cryptic as some of Ian's usual offerings. It seems the protagonist is grappling with unrequited love, mustering the courage to approach the woman he admires, only to face rejection.

The heartbreak is palpable as he arrives "cap in hand", hoping to win her over, but discovers she's already set the table for another man. Although he can now retreat, replacing his cap on his head, it offers little solace. Such melancholic endings are characteristic of Ian's lyrical style.

"Pibroch (Cap In Hand)" has been played live over the years, sometimes as an instrumental for Martin to work out on, sometimes in shortened from in combination with other songs like "Pussy Willow" or "Black Satin Dancer".

I think of this track as being about as typical of Tull as you can get. It embodies the lengthy symphonic sound often found on their albums, blending rock, classical, and Celtic folk elements with captivating lyrics and superb vocals. Clocking in at eight minutes and thirty-three seconds, it encapsulates Tull's signature style remarkably well.

Despite the absence of actual bagpipes, the instrumental aspect earns a solid 7/10, while the lyrical content scores a commendable 9/10. Overall, it averages out to an impressive 8/10 rating. Not bad for a song that should and could have featured bagpipes. All the same, it turned out well.

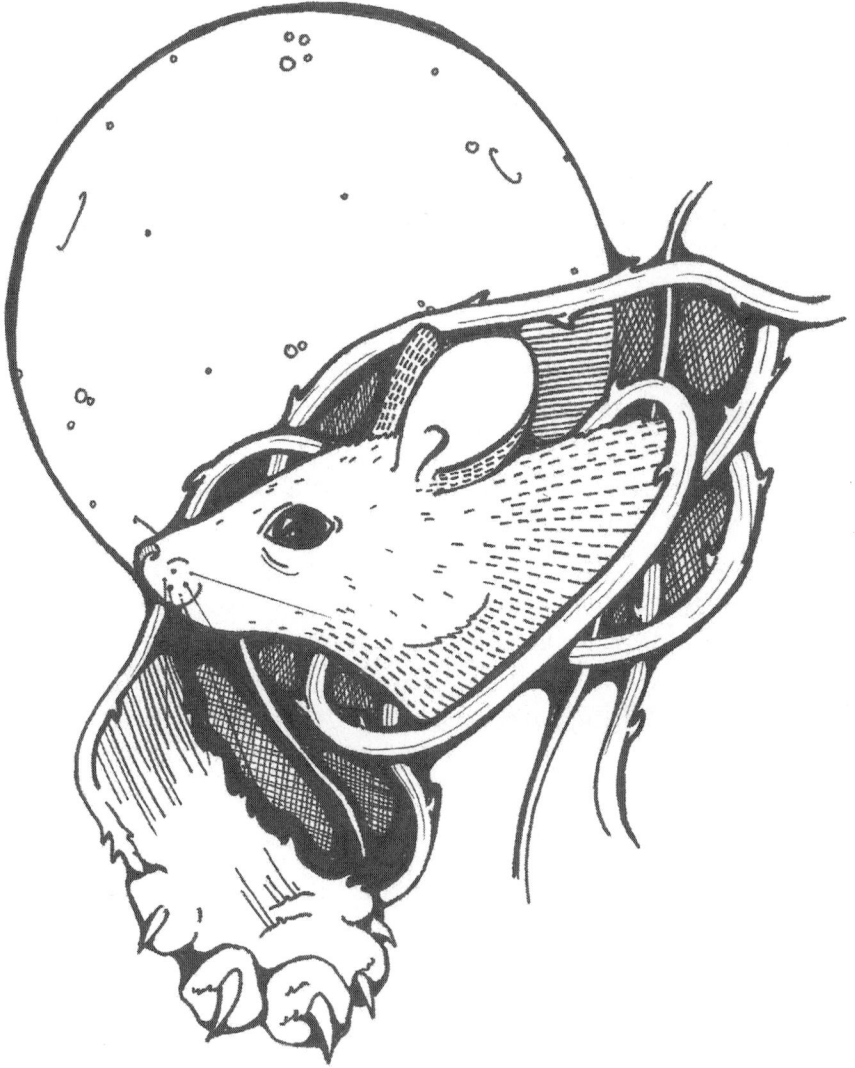

17.
And The Mouse Police Never Sleeps...
It's just not punk

The year 1978 was dominated by the rise of punk. Some albums released that year included *Give 'Em Enough Rope* by The Clash, *Public Image Ltd* by Public Image (John Lydon), *The Scream* by Siouxsie and the Banshees, and *All Mod Cons* by The Jam.

In the midst of all this punk and new wave exuberance, Jethro Tull, considered by many to be rock dinosaurs by this point, released an album focused on large horses and rural life.

On the cover of *Heavy Horses*, Ian sported a cravat and tweeds, while the back cover featured band members with bowties, football boots, and red wine.

The band's hair was possibly a bit shorter to align with the prevailing anti-fashion trends of the time. Both manager Terry Ellis and Chrysalis Records head Chris Wright had advised Ian that Tull should appeal to the masses with songs about relationships and cars, or perhaps anarchist diatribes.

To his credit, Ian stuck to his unique vision with songs about shire horses ("Heavy Horses"), trains ("Journeyman"), winged insects ("Moths"), and the Winged Isle ("Acres Wild"). There was even a song about a cat named Mistletoe, who eats vermin for a living.

There are plenty of songs with "cat" in the title, but few about actual felines. A "cool cat" refers to a fashionable or hip person, with no feline characteristics at all; "Cool For Cats" by

Squeeze falls into this category.

A pussycat can be a mild-mannered character featured in many songs, but this is not the stereotypical subject matter Ian Anderson would focus on. He has written at least four songs about real cats: "And The Mouse Police Never Sleeps...", "Hunt By Numbers" from *J-Tull Dot Com*, and Rupi's Dance" and "Old Black Cat" from the Rupi's Dance solo album.

Ian has supported various cat charities over the years, so it's safe to conclude that he is quite fond of cats. To the best of my knowledge, he has not yet written a song about goldfish.

"And the Mouse Police Never Sleeps..." is the opening track of the *Heavy Horses* album, recorded in January 1978 at Maison Rouge Studio in Fulham, London, and released in April 1978.

The song is about three minutes and twenty seconds long. Instrumentally, it stands out from other Tull songs due to its amazing stop-start, jerky rhythm that still manages to flow seamlessly, making it irresistibly foot-tapping.

Ian Anderson claims the rhythm is based on a drum pattern from "Click Clack" by Artie Tripp, who was the drummer for Captain Beefheart in the early seventiess.

Captain Beefheart had toured with Tull, and Barrie Barlow was familiar with the drum pattern, incorporating it into "The Mouse Police Never Sleeps...". After repeated listens and some help from my syncopated wife (a classically trained musician), we believe the track is partly in 6/8 time, although we could be wrong.

David Palmer, another classically trained musician, claims to have written and incorporated a "fugue connection" based on "Three Blind Mice", although I can't quite discern it. Additionally, Ian was experiencing some vocal problems at the time, but his rough, gravelly, smoker's voice adds to the rural tone of this and other tracks on *Heavy Horses*.

Lyrically, the song is about a cat that Ian Anderson had named Mistletoe. While Mistletoe could be pleasant and purr while sitting on a lap, she was also a ruthless hunter of mice and rats around the Anderson household. The straightforward and entertaining lyrics capture the essence of this little "mouse police" monster of a cat.

The song has not been played live often, if at all. It is not included on the *Bursting Out* live album, nor did I see Tull perform it during their Manchester gig while touring with *Heavy Horses* in 1978. However, the track was well received by critics, fans, and cats alike and would have probably been well received if played live.

This is a strange one for me. I am indifferent to cats and didn't really catch on to this song for the first forty-odd years after its release, considering it just another album track.

Around 2020, I suddenly thought, "Wow, what have I missed?". I am now fond of the track instrumentally, as it really showcases what a great drummer Barrie was for Tull. The time signature and rhythm really do it for me.

In the mid-seventies, a notable exponent of the art and "quiet" drummer, John Bonham, called Barrie "the greatest rock drummer England ever produced".

Therefore, I think 7/10 for the feline song lyrics, 8/10 for the music track, and 10/10 for Barriemore Barlow, drummer extraordinaire. This averages out to... a pretty good mark!

18.
Weathercock
It's just not heavy but it's made of metal

"Weathercock" is the second song I've chosen from *Heavy Horses*, an album that many consider to be Tull's best. For me, it would be in my top twenty-three, but towards the upper end.

I could have picked "Rover" or "Acres Wild" as my second song from the album, as I love both. They evocatively suggest wild Scottish landscapes with romantic encounters in the summer months.

However, I chose the winter song "Weathercock" instead. My other choice from *Heavy Horses*, "And The Mouse Police Never Sleeps...", bookends the album at the start, with "Weathercock" at the end. There is also a second version of "Weathercock" on *The Jethro Tull Christmas Album* from 2003.

"Weathercock" is introduced lyrically in "And The Mouse Police Never Sleeps..." as a "windy rooftop weathercock" at the end of the song. This makes sense because weathercocks, or wind vanes, are typically found on rooftops, often on churches or barns.

They show wind direction and are usually decorative, often featuring a cockerel atop a structure with four compass points. Sometimes, they have designs like ships, arrows, or horses instead of a cockerel. The head of the cockerel or arrow points in the direction of the wind.

Weathercocks are still found on many church steeples in

the UK today and can symbolise the clergy or priests calling people to prayer. Beyond their practical use of indicating wind direction, they are part of English folklore, representing tradition, comfort, and protection, as they can signal changing weather. There are even Weathercock inns and pubs. Only *Songs From The Wood* or *Heavy Horses* could have included a song like this.

The lyrics of "Weathercock" speak of the weathercock standing worthy and proud against all sorts of weather: "did the cold winds bite you, did you face up to the fright", while also offering protection and comfort with lines like "do you fight the rush of winter, do you hold snowflakes at bay".

In the choruses, the weathercock seems to have the power to influence the weather, "to make this day bright" and bring "the best of good will".

The weathercock serves as both a protector from harsh weather and a bringer of fair weather, reflecting some of Ian Anderson's more joyous and optimistic lyrics. It's a warm song for a cold winter's day.

Perhaps no band of a metallic persuasion could get away with this song, but Jethro Tull can, because, lyrically, there are never any boundaries. Besides, this was the period of Ian's rustic, folksy, green phase of composition.

"Weathercock" delivers everything you could ever want from Tull instrumentally. It begins gently with acoustic tones and a captivating melody. Ian's singing, with the slight gruffness in his voice, adds drama.

Then comes a mid-song flute solo, followed by another verse, and suddenly, the track takes off into the rock 'n' roll stratosphere. Martin's fantastic solo intertwines seamlessly with Ian's flute, creating one of the top guitar and flute outros in the Tull song catalogue.

The version of "Weathercock" featured on *The Jethro Tull Christmas Album* maintains a similar arrangement to the original. However, Ian's more delicate voice from 2003 adds to the melancholic feel of the song.

Unlike in "Weathercock" from *Heavy Horses*, there isn't quite the same guitar/flute interaction at the end. This might be because the instruments were recorded separately in different locations and added together later in the studio. In contrast, the earlier version feels more natural and spontaneous.

Personally, I prefer the original "Weathercock" on *Heavy Horses*. The version on *The Jethro Tull Christmas Album* feels more controlled and contrived to me, lacking the looseness and flair of the original. Therefore, "Weathercock" (2) gets a 7/10, while "Weathercock" (1) gets a 9/10.

19.
Dun Ringill
A Scottish "Yesterday"

It's important to begin this chapter with a mention of someone who did not play on "Dun Ringill" and maybe should have done — John Glasscock.

John only played on three tracks from *Stormwatch*: "Orion", "Flying Dutchman", and "Elegy". The challenges and tragic end of John's life have been extensively covered in various Tull biographies (refer to the bibliography for more details).

By the spring of 1979, John's health had deteriorated significantly. Dental treatment in 1978 for a tooth abscess, followed by surgery for a hereditary heart condition, had taken a toll on him. He couldn't join the *Heavy Horses* tour due to his health issues and was replaced by Tony Williams from Blackpool, a friend of Barrie's, for live performances on bass.

John was by all accounts a wonderful gregarious charming man who could not say no to a party or a drink too many. Unfortunately, his rock 'n' roll lifestyle didn't help his health.

During the *Stormwatch* recordings, John's condition worsened, affecting his playing ability. Ian eventually suggested or insisted that he take time off to recuperate and return to the band when he felt better.

Dave Pegg filled in for him during most of the *Stormwatch* tours in 1979. Despite some debate over whether more could have been done to assist John, his health continued to decline. He very sadly passed away on 17th November 1979. He was only twenty-eight.

By 1979, Ian had bought a second rural estate, this time

on the Isle of Skye at Kilmarie. This new environment had a significant impact on the themes explored in *Stormwatch*, with the sea, weather, and environmental concerns all playing a part.

Ironically, despite the album's thematic inspiration, the recording process itself took place in the urban setting of London, at the Maison Rouge Studios, spanning from summer 1978 to spring 1979.

"Dun Ringill" stands out as one of the quintessential Jethro Tull tracks, resonating deeply with many fans, including myself.

Unlike "Baker St Muse", which is grounded in the urban landscape of London, this song transports us to a faraway rustic place. As Ian shifted his primary domestic location to the Isle of Skye in the late seventies, Dun Ringill became a focal point of inspiration.

It's a real location, far more intriguing to write about than the nondescript sheds that most of us might have in our gardens.

Dun Ringill, an ancient hill fort, has a history spanning over a millennium. Once the seat of the Clan Mackinnon, it holds the echoes of ancient times, where one could almost envision "the old gods play". Amidst this mystical backdrop, the lyrics hint at a shifting weather pattern, adding to the atmospheric allure of the song.

In the late 1980s, the BBC's main weatherman was John Kettley, immortalised in the novelty single "John Kettley Is A Weather Man" by A Tribe of Toffs in 1988.

But even before Kettley, another weatherman had a small yet noteworthy role in rock history. Francis Wilson, employed by Thames TV in 1978, garnered attention for his casual attire — a look that stood out among the typically conservative weather presenters of the time.

His non-meteorology jeans and open-shirt style made him something of a trendsetter, earning him fan mail and recognition. Wilson's role on the *Stormwatch* album was a testament to his trendy persona. He lent his voice to the spoken word introduction of "Dun Ringill" and read the shipping forecast on "North Sea Oil".

When I first heard "Dun Ringill" years ago, I was absolutely captivated by it. It's a challenge to choose Jethro Tull's best acoustic guitar-based song. Could it be "Life Is A Long Song",

"One White Duck/O10=Nothing at All", "Jack In The Green", "Under Wraps", or even "Broadford Bazaar" from the *Stormwatch* box set?

"Dun Ringill" is definitely among the top contenders. I sometimes liken it to Jethro Tull's "Yesterday" — a melody plucked from the ether that, like The Beatles' song, was never released as a single but gained immense popularity over time. Both songs are acoustic pieces from bands primarily known for amplified instruments.

"Dun Ringill" is said to feature cyclical chord changes, transitioning from 6/8 in the verses to 3/4 in the choruses. Whatever the technicalities, it resonates deeply with me.

Interestingly, "Dun Ringill" has also left its mark on the Swedish prog metal band Opeth. According to band member Mikael Åkerfeldt, their 2016 track "Will O The Wisp" is a direct descendant of "Dun Ringill", featuring a catchy melody paired with dark lyrics.

Lyrically, "Dun Ringill" is one of those Tull songs that I struggle to fully grasp. The introductory spoken words by Francis Wilson, echoed by Ian, are particularly poetic and captivating, evoking imagery of the crashing sea against the windy shore — a fitting scene for Dun Ringill fort, situated along the coast.

Where the subsequent lyrics revolve around rendezvousing at Dun Ringill and observing the "old gods at play" amidst stormy weather, I wonder whether they are perhaps hinting at deeper existential themes.

Like many Tull songs, there's a myriad of interpretations circulating online, some profound and others a bit dubious. All the same, the elusive quality of "Dun Ringill" adds to its otherworldly charm and entertainment value. It's almost as if the "old gods" themselves were definitely playing in bestowing this song upon Ian Anderson.

"Dun Ringill" was performed live during the Stormwatch tours and sporadically in the 1980s, often featuring Martin's tasteful acoustic guitar leads layered over Ian's cyclical chords.

Additionally, Ian performed the song in the 1981 Slipstream video, albeit not at Dun Ringill fort, but against the backdrop of the White Cliffs of Dover — a location that, to my knowledge, hasn't inspired a Tull song.

"Dun Ringill" has found its way onto numerous compilations and "best of" collections. It is rumoured to be the favourite Tull song of Andy Giddings, the band's keyboard player during the 1990s and early 2000s.

Interestingly, a Swedish band called Dun Ringill, formed in 2017, released a concept album titled Where The Old Gods Play Act 1 & 2, with the lead track "Awakening" featuring sea and seagull sounds before diving into heavy metal riffing.

While this bears no direct connection to our beloved "Dun Ringill" by Jethro Tull, it's fascinating how the influence of a Scottish hill fort and a forty-five-year-old song from Tull legends can reach a contemporary Swedish metal band. Who would have thought it?

As you may well have gathered, I just absolutely love this song! Could it be the best Tull song ever? Wait and find out. It is a monstrously ridiculous 11/10 from me.

20.
The Pine Marten's Jig
It's just not folk

The year 1980 was the time of Jethro Tull's infamous big split. Here's a condensed version of what happened: The British band UK had toured with Tull in 1979, leaving Ian Anderson impressed by the talents of keyboard and violin virtuoso Eddie Jobson, known for his work with Roxy Music and musical polymath Frank Zappa.

Ian and Eddie planned to collaborate on an Ian Anderson solo album. Meanwhile, Barrie was considering leaving Tull, and John and David were exploring a classical/rock crossover project called Tallis.

Ian enlisted Dave Pegg for the solo album, bringing in Eddie's friend Mark Craney on drums. After some persuasion, Martin Barre joined in for guitar work on the Anderson tapes. However, Chrysalis Records doubted the success of a solo Anderson album and insisted it be released under the Jethro Tull name.

This decision led to complications. A letter from the record company effectively dismissed John Evan, Barrie Barlow, and David Palmer. Consequently, the Anderson-Jobson-Craney-Pegg-Barre line-up released the album as a Jethro Tull record rather than an Ian Anderson solo project. This move stirred up resentment and discord among the band members. Ian later apologised, and a semblance of peace was restored.

Unfortunately, Barrie and John never collaborated with Ian or Tull again. However, David would involve Ian in some of his orchestral rock endeavours in the late 1980s.

The 1970s had been a golden era for Tull as a cohesive unit. Despite a change in bass player and the addition of David, the line-up had remained stable, harmonious, and mostly content.

However, as the 1980s dawned, some fans and critics claimed that Tull had devolved into Ian and a rotating cast of supporting musicians. Yet, Ian had always been the band's primary songwriter, lead arranger, vocalist, and, notably, flute player since its inception. This leadership would continue into the 1980s and beyond, producing some remarkable music despite the changing line-ups.

While some may have lost faith in Tull at the beginning of the eighties, I believe there were still moments of brilliance and collective musicality among the various iterations of the band that followed.

For instance, Martin Barre's continued presence until 2011 stands as a testament to the enduring quality of Tull's output. Essentially, the first album of the 1980s, in my opinion, was more than halfway decent.

A charming little tune emerged on the *A* album that harkened back to the folksy vibe of *Songs From The Wood*. This marks the third and final instrumental on our list. "The Pine Marten's Jig" is a lively blend of twiddly, fiddly, folksy, rocky, and flutey elements, with a distinctly jiggy feel. Interestingly, it's the only Tull track to feature "Jig" in the title.

A jig is a spirited folk dance typically set in compound meter, often in 12/8 time, although 6/8 and 9/8 signatures can also be used.

In simpler terms, it's the kind of music that's perfect for dancing to when you're syncopatingly drunk! But how does a jig differ from a reel? Well, while a reel is typically counted in four, a jig is counted in three. Time signatures can be as elusive as some of Ian's lyrics, but jigs and reels are undeniably good fun to listen to.

One of the most well-known rock tracks featuring a jig is "Jig A Jig" by East of Eden in 1970, which combines three traditional reels ("The Ashplant Reel", "Jenny's Chicken" and "Drowsy Maggie") with a violin leading over a rock backing.

Jethro Tull also dabbled in jigs, with "Drowsy Maggie" showcased in the 1980s as a platform for Dave Pegg's mandolin skills. They sometimes fused it with "The Pine Marten's Jig".

The band had previously explored jig elements in "Passion Jig" from *A Passion Play* and "Pibroch (Cap In Hand)" from *Songs From The Wood*, as well as "Flying Dutchman" from *Stormwatch*.

Given Tull's history in this area, "The Pine Marten's Jig" might have been a nod to welcoming ex-Fairport Convention folkie Dave Pegg into the fold.

A pine marten, akin to Ian's cat Mistletoe in "The Mouse Police Never Sleeps...", is a small, carnivorous mammal commonly found in the rustic terrains of Skye and Northwest Scotland. Ian probably encountered them during his time there. "The Pine Marten's Jig" emerged as part of the *A* album, recorded in summer 1980 and released in September of the same year.

Instrumentally, the track is a captivating blend of traditional folk and hard rock, all packed into a concise three minutes and twenty-nine seconds. The first minute and six seconds feature lively, folk-inspired music driven by flute, mandolin, and violin, accompanied by a pulsating rhythm section of bass and drums. This is followed by a brief, electrifying solo, reminiscent of either a violin or guitar, that adds an unexpected twist to the mix.

At one minute and thirty seconds, a flute solo takes centre stage, supported by rhythmic violin, before giving way to what seems to be a definite guitar solo.

The track then transitions into more playful fiddling, leading back to the main jig from two minutes and fifty-seven seconds until the end. It's like a miniature folk-rock symphony, with a prog rock vibe that's both epic and enthralling.

As an instrumental piece, there are no intellectual, metaphor-laden Anderson lyrics to dissect, making it a refreshing change. Overall, "The Pine Marten's Jig" stands out as a remarkably well-executed composition.

Tull performed "The Pine Marten's Jig" live during the A tours, albeit with some apprehension, as Ian noted it was "fiendishly difficult to play". Personally, it sounds fine to me. A live rendition can be found on the *A* box set. In subsequent tours, it was often paired with "Drowsy Maggie", as mentioned earlier.

Without beating about the bush or the jig, I do rather like this track. I would put it ahead of "Dharma For One" but just behind "Bourée" as my favourite Tull instrumental. Therefore, I will give it a bouncy little score of 8/10.

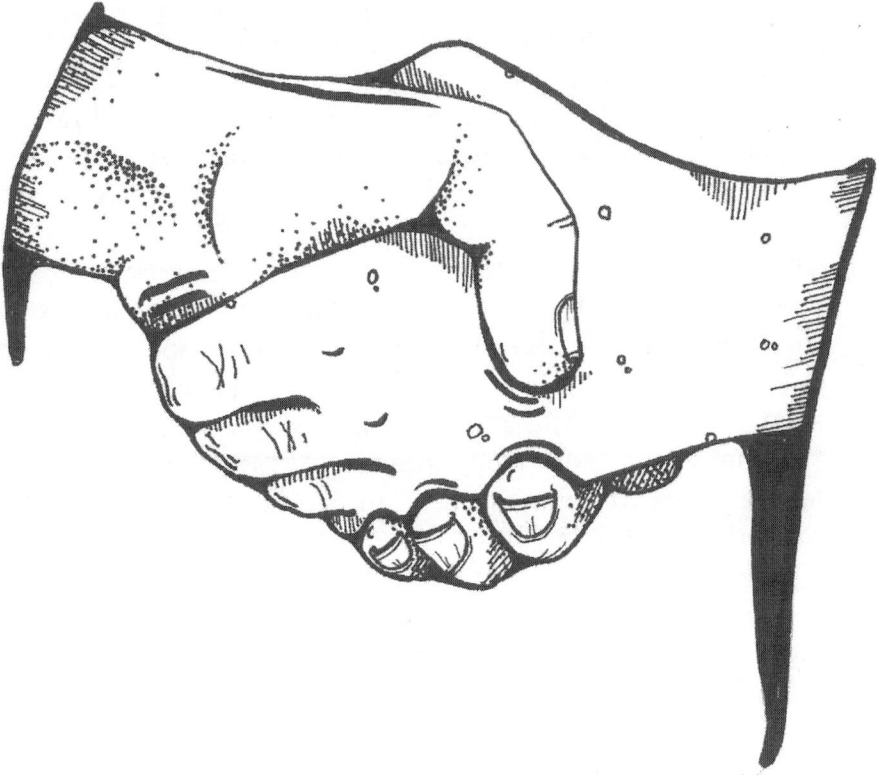

21.
Clasp
Handshakes are for real?

The handshake has long been a traditional form of greeting, symbolising friendly intentions by showing that no weapons are held. Of course, this doesn't account for ambivalently ambidextrous individuals who might still be capable of harm with their other hand. Handshakes are also used to convey congratulations after a sporting event or political election.

There are different styles of handshakes: the firm, eye-contacting grip favoured by alpha males, which is not ideal for the delicate hands of our favourite flute player; and the weak, sweaty palm touch typical of shy and introverted individuals who avoid eye contact.

The ideal handshake is firm but fair, striking a balance between the two extremes. For those interested in records, the longest handshake lasted over fifteen hours. However, it's worth noting that handshakes are also an effective way to spread germs.

Alternatively, there is always the fist bump or, even better, rubbing elbows, a greeting preferred by sensitive flute players. "To rub elbows with" is an American phrase meaning to meet and associate with people. However, taking it literally offers a practical alternative: it protects hands from the wear and tear of handshakes, reduces germ transfer, and remains a friendly, if slightly eccentric, greeting.

Ian Anderson embraced this tradition so thoroughly that he even named some of his solo performing and speaking gigs in the USA in the 2000s "The Rubbing Elbows Tours".

Given his inventive spirit, it is natural that Ian would write a song about the trials and tribulations of the handshake, even before he popularised "rubbing elbows".

For years, I thought the song in question was called "The Clasp", as in "the handshake".

However, while starting this chapter, I finally realised that the definitive article is missing; it's simply "Clasp", as in just "handshake". And I thought I was a proper Tullite!

By 1982, more changes had occurred in Jethro Tull. Special guest Eddie Jobson had left, as had drummer Mark Craney, who wanted to base himself in the USA. New drummer Gerry Conway, who had worked with Cat Stevens among others, joined the band. Conway was a more straightforward, less intricate drummer than Craney, which was what Ian wanted at the time.

Initially, for the *Broadsword And The Beast* album, Ian worked with modern keyboards himself. However, he eventually realised he needed a classically trained, technologically literate, all-around superstar keyboard player.

They found Peter-John Vitesse, who looked about ten years old but played piano and every other conceivable keyboard like an old pro. The new band gelled quickly, with the help of outside producer Paul Samwell-Smith, formerly of The Yardbirds. The album was recorded over the winter of 1981-82 and released in April 1982. "Clasp" was played live on the Broadsword And The Beast tours that followed.

There have been several songs about handshakes over the years, such as The White Stripes' "Let's Shake Hands" and Nickelback's "Shakin' Hands", but neither bear any stylistic or lyrical resemblance to Jethro Tull's "Clasp".

Instrumentally, "Clasp" is a blend of old and new. The track is dominated by keyboards and synthesised voice treatments using vocoders, featuring lots of eighties technology with just a hint of centuries-old flute. The great strength of this track, like much of Tull's music, is its ability to sound modern and up to date while simultaneously feeling mysteriously ancient and historically profound.

Lyrically, "Clasp" conveys Ian Anderson's observations on the handshake, emphasising its positive aspects. It serves as a welcoming gesture, encouraging people to "make the clasp" more often and not be afraid to reach out.

However, true to his nuanced style, Ian concludes with a cautionary note: "exchange the lie, pretend to make the clasp". This suggests we should avoid shaking hands and making agreements with insincere or bad people.

Ian is well known for preferring to literally rub elbows, protecting his flute-playing fingers, and avoiding the clasp of a handshake. He claims to have invented the practice of physically rubbing elbows, although it's uncertain if posterity will remember this.

Playing the flute in a rock band and writing some of the best songs of all time, in many people's eyes and ears, may be his true legacy. At least Ian is not claiming to have invented the handshake.

It's cliché time again. I do love this one musically and lyrically (don't worry, I don't love the next song in the next chapter, quite the opposite). Therefore, I award 3/5 for the lyrics and 4/5 for the music, giving a total of 8/10. Words and sums fail me!

22.
Apogee
In space toilet arrangements

Under Wraps, released in 1984, is a much-maligned album by both fans and critics, and I was no exception. However, after listening to the whole album again while preparing for this chapter, I realised it's not half good, which means it's not half bad either.

There are some great songs on it, including one of the best Tull acoustic tracks of all time. Ian Anderson's voice was at the height of its powers for a short period, and there's even more flute on the tracks than I previously thought. However, someone could perhaps come along and just shoot the *****y drum machine!

After the Broadsword And The Beast tours, drummer Gerry Conway left the band. Ian Anderson recorded the solo album *Walk Into Light* with assistance from Peter-John Vitesse, but without a human drummer.

The early 1980s were awash with new music technology, which was being exploited by new wave bands and also integrated into the sounds of older bands like Yes, Genesis, and Jethro Tull to bring their music up to date.

When Tull reconvened for the *Under Wraps* album in spring 1984, the drumming duties were taken over by "Mr. A. Linn Drum" (Linn being the brand of the drum machine). This machine was metronomically and monotonously precise, never ahead or behind the beat, and never asking for a pay raise. However, "Mr. A. Linn Drum" also played with no feel, no soul, and almost no paradiddles.

It remains unclear as to why Ian decided to use a drum machine for the album. It seemed to be an experiment — a "let's give it a go" moment — that ultimately did not work for Tull.

Genesis and Phil Collins also used drum machines, but Phil would drum and embellish over the mechanised beat, as exemplified in the Genesis song "Mama" or his solo hit "In The Air Tonight".

Tull did eventually produce one outstanding track with a drum machine and no real drummer: "Steel Monkey" from the *Crest Of A Knave* album (see chapter 24). Ian has since expressed a desire to redo the album with a real drummer, and I'm sure he would get plenty of volunteers. Doane Perry joined to play real drums for the Under Wraps tour.

Great songs on the album include the acoustic "Under Wraps" (2), "Heat", a mini prog monstrosity of epic proportions, and "European Legacy", which always reminds me of "Every Breath You Take" by The Police, which is no bad thing.

However, there are some stinkers on the album as well. I apologise to "Apogee", which, even on a good day, sort of fits into that category.

An Apogee signifies "the highest point", whether in a career or the furthest point in a spaceship's orbit around Earth or another celestial body. In the Tull song, it's the spaceship's "Apogee".

The lyrics are intriguing, and as usual, I don't quite grasp them. Perhaps it's about the loneliness experienced in space, at the apogee of the furthest distance from Earth, feeling isolated from family and friends. Amidst all of this, Ian humorously reminds the astronauts not to forget the basics, like urinating — an entertaining line with excellent advice.

Tennyson and Wordsworth are mentioned in the lyrics, although I'm not entirely sure why. Maybe their works were to be read in space. My conclusion is that the lyrics are meant to be bizarre, fun, and weird. However, Elton John does it better with "Rocket Man", as does Major Tom and David Bowie in "Space Oddity".

Peter-John Vitesse is credited as a co-writer here, indicating a significant influence on the music and instrumentation, which includes slashing guitar, synthesised keyboards, and Ian singing in a high register — all promising elements.

However, "Mr. A. Linn Drum" just doesn't resonate with me, and it's not one of Ian's or Peter's best melodies. It's disheartening to realise how much I generally love Tull yet struggle to relate to and enjoy this track. Therefore, I can only award it a 2/10.

However, all is not lost! As mentioned earlier, upon listening very carefully to the *Under Wraps* album as a whole, I've discovered nuances, subtleties, mini-melodies, and trilling flutes that went unnoticed before.

That said, should Ian go ahead and re-record or add a real drummer to the album, I would welcome it. Among the other songs, "Under Wraps" (2) would get a 10/10 (see chapter 23), "Heat" would receive a 9/10, and "European Legacy" an 8/10. "Saboteur", with a little more flute, is a hidden gem that could earn a 7/10. Meanwhile, I'm taking drumming lessons, just in case I get the call...

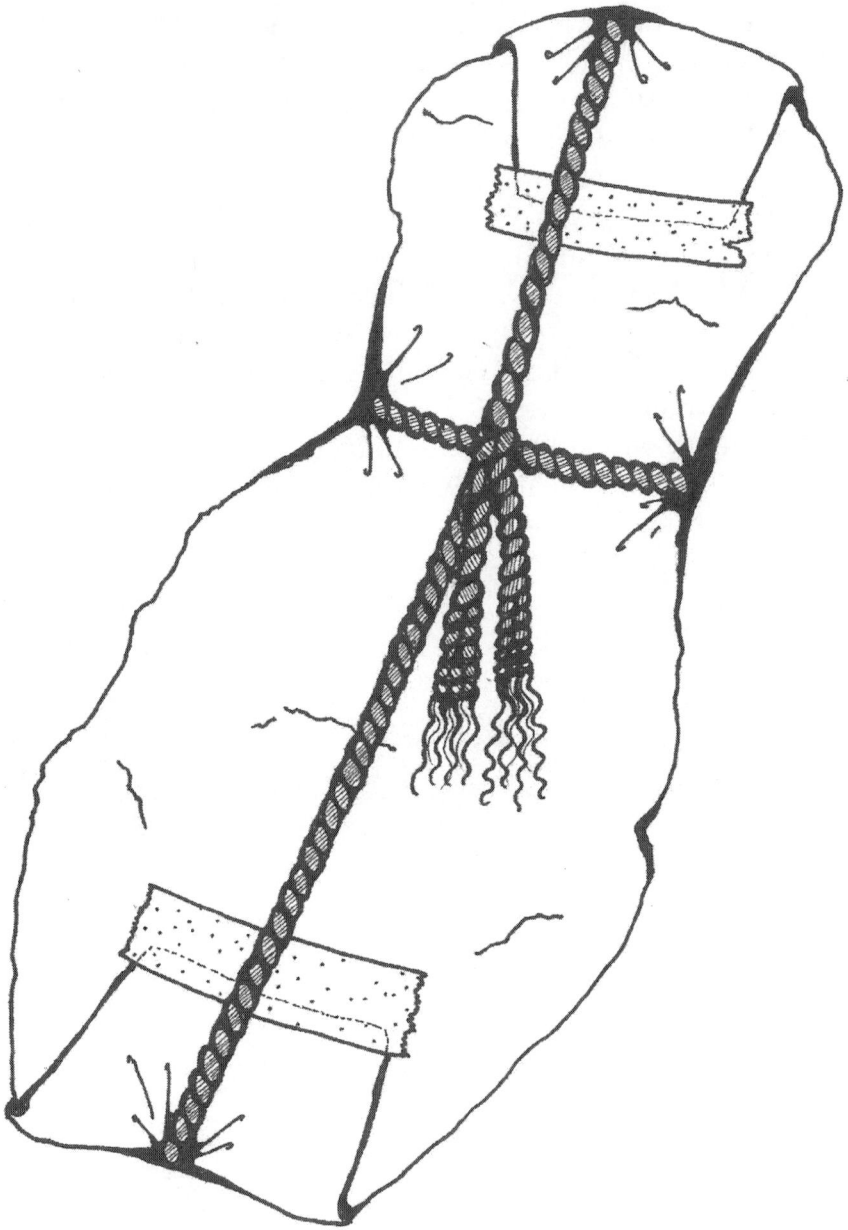

114

23.
Under Wraps
It's just not a drum machine

By 1984, Ian Anderson was approaching the age of thirty-seven. Since 1968, he had been playing the flute and singing in Jethro Tull. By the end of 1984, Tull had performed 1,365 concerts — a considerable amount of singing and flute-playing without even a cigarette break.

Yet, during the recording of the *Under Wraps* album in 1984, Ian's vocal abilities were still strong. He himself has admitted that even in those earlier years, he didn't consider himself to have much of a singing voice. However, in my opinion, no one else could have sung Tull songs as well as he did.

This holds true for the entirety of Tull's catalogue, not just before 1984. In later years, his thinner voice suited the post-1984 songs well, as the arrangements and compositions adjusted to accommodate his more limited vocals.

Meanwhile, in a parallel universe where Tony Iommi permanently joined Jethro Sabbath, imagine if the magnificent tenor of Yes' Jon Anderson had joined the band on vocals. It's difficult to imagine him wrapping his vocal chords around "Thick As A Brick".

Similarly, I can't envision Ian Anderson baritoning his way through "Close To The Edge", although I'm sure he could have delivered a mighty flute solo! Even today, Ian can successfully sing any Tull song, most of the time. When I look at cover versions of Tull songs on the Internet, they just don't sound right with other people singing them.

However, the demanding tracks from *Under Wraps* took a

toll on Ian's singing. On the electronic studio version of "Under Wraps" (1), Ian pushed his vocals to the limit. Recreating the higher vocals live was even more challenging.

During the late 1984 Under Wraps tour, Ian's voice finally gave out during a series of concerts in Australia. Some shows had to be cancelled, and Ian, under doctor's orders, was instructed to rest his voice for a year throughout 1985.

When he and Tull returned with *Crest Of A Knave* in 1987, his voice had changed. He remained an effective singer for Tull, but over the subsequent years, his singing voice posed challenges (more details on these vocal issues can be found in the conclusion chapter). However, when he recorded the track(s) "Under Wraps", his singing voice was still powerful, strong, and resonant.

Now we're going to indulge in a bit of cheating because there are two versions of "Under Wraps" – one electronic and rocky, and the other exquisitely folksy. Despite sharing the same lyrics and chord sequences, they sound completely different. So, let's take a look at both.

In both versions of "Under Wraps", the verses explore the theme of sleeping with the enemy, akin to James Bond meeting Jethro Tull as a super spy in rock band form. It's fun stuff and not too deep for me to understand, I hope.

"Under Wraps" (1) is a synthetic, synthesised track with a hint of crunchy guitar, where Ian really pushes his upper tonal boundaries in singing.

When it was performed live, Martin's guitar took a more prominent role, giving it a vibe reminiscent of ZZ Top meets Thomas Dolby on a particularly good beard day.

The presence of "Mr. A. Linn Drum" is regrettable, but at least Doane Perry, a real drummer with his own DNA, took over on live drums for this track during the Under Wraps tours later in 1984.

After extensive research, it's challenging to find fans and reviewers who think this version is even halfway decent. Most people don't like it. Rightly or wrongly, Peter-John Vitesse gets the blame for the anaemic, emotionless arrangement, but it's worth noting that Ian wrote the track on his own and gave Peter the freedom to assist in constructing songs.

"Under Wraps" (2) takes on a vastly different tone. With acoustic guitar chording, a double bass, tambourine, and a delightful sequence of single notes on acoustic guitar, the arrangement and mood shift entirely.

This version exudes warmth and emotional resonance, a stark departure from the synthetic feel of version (1). It serves as a reminder that Tull can still evoke the essence of *Songs From The Wood*, utilising wooden, non-amplified instruments.

In my opinion, Ian sounds better vocally on this track than on any other Tull song! Critics and fans alike responded with overwhelmingly positive reactions to "Under Wraps" (2), in stark contrast to version (1).

In my view, "Under Wraps" (1) earns a modest 5/10. If real drumming were to replace the artificial beats, it might elevate the score to a 7/10 in the future. On the other hand, "Under Wraps" (2) effortlessly secures a perfect 10/10, claiming a top spot in Tull's acoustic repertoire.

© Bekah Elliott

24.
Steel Monkey
Eat your heart out, Metallica!

*C*rest Of A Knave was recorded in spring 1987 and released in September of the same year. Following his severe throat issues in 1984, Ian took a hiatus from Tull activities for about eighteen months.

When he returned to singing, he had adopted a lower vocal register, reminiscent of Mark Knopfler's style, and delivered songs with a gentle, spoken-sung approach. Some tracks, like "She Said She Was A Dancer", even bore a resemblance to Dire Straits, especially with Martin's guitar work echoing Mark's signature style in his solos.

However, the album as a whole took a decidedly rocking direction, with electric guitars taking centre stage, and Martin's playing reaching new heights, showcasing impeccable solos and arrangements.

Ian contributed keyboards, allowing Martin's guitar work to shine even more. The rhythm section featured both Gerry Conway and newcomer Doane Perry on drums, with Dave Pegg providing solid bass throughout.

Despite this shift towards a more electric sound, Crest Of A Knave still retained elements of quintessential Tull, blending acoustic guitars, flutes, and folk influences with prog rock epics like "Budapest" and "Farm On The Freeway".

Notably, the original version of "Budapest" stretched to a staggering twenty-two minutes at one point.

Ultimately, Crest Of A Knave marked a triumphant return to form for Tull, earning critical acclaim and even winning a

Grammy for Best Hard Rock/Metal Recording in 1989.

The story and controversy surrounding Jethro Tull's Grammy win for Best Hard Rock/Metal Recording over Metallica's *And Justice For All* is well-known and doesn't need to be recounted here in detail.

However, it's worth noting that despite this recognition, Jethro Tull has still not been inducted into the Rock And Roll Hall Of Fame, making the Grammy win a sort of compensation for a lifetime of musical achievement.

Interestingly, Tull's record company, Chrysalis, humorously advertised the gold flute as a "heavy metal instrument" following the awards ceremony.

If any song from the album contributed to this unexpected win, it could arguably be "Steel Monkey".

In chapter 11, in discussing "The Story Of The Hare Who Lost His Spectacles", I mentioned how it's remarkable that the same band could release such a whimsical piece and then, thirteen years later, put out "Steel Monkey".

This duality is part of what makes Tull unique. Despite both tracks having accompanying videos, they diverge significantly beyond that point.

When I think of this track, I can't help but recall the iconic 1932 photograph, "Lunch Atop A Skyscraper", depicting eleven steelworkers casually dining on a beam eight hundred feet above New York City during the construction of the Rockefeller Centre.

Not a safety harness or high-visibility jacket in sight — those were the days! In the "Steel Monkey" music video, Ian, Martin, and Dave roamed around on a slightly smaller metal structure, exuding a similarly cool aura. The song's imagery is all about toughness, bravery, and masculinity — the perfect recipe for some hard-hitting heavy metal.

It's no wonder Tull snagged that Grammy. But whatever happened to the gentle, rural vibes of songs like "Dun Ringill"? The point is, Jethro Tull encompassed heavy metal, folksy acoustic, and much more. Could Metallica pull off a blistering rendition of "Dun Ringill"? That would surely be a challenge for Lars, James, Kirk, and Robert in the style of "Nothing Else Matters" please.

Lyrically, the message in "Steel Monkey" is perhaps the most straightforward in the entire Tull repertoire. To me, it's saying, "I'm a high-rise, heavy metal, steel monkey: I feel no pain, so don't mess with me".

I appreciate the nod to the "monkey puzzle" tree in the lyrics — a personal favourite of mine — but I'm not entirely sure if Ian was drawing an arboreal connection at that particular moment in the first verse.

Musically, "Steel Monkey" relies on a synthesised rhythm and a skilfully utilised drum machine, a far cry from the shortcomings of "Mr. A. Linn Drum" on *Under Wraps*.

These elements form the foundation of the track, over which Ian sings while Martin delivers an impressive series of solos. I've witnessed the song performed live, sometimes with Ian adding a second guitar or going hands-free, all while sporting heavy metal shades.

The track was released as a single, reaching number 84 in the US and remaining in the top 100 for four weeks. Both fans and critics reacted positively, acknowledging that even after nearly twenty years, Tull could still deliver a rocking performance.

"Steel Monkey" has become my favourite Tull song, that doesn't include flute. It is an "everything louder than everything else", heavy metal monster, getting 9/10 from me.

122

25.
Jack-A-Lynn
Versions thereof

A box set in music is a collection of related recordings that share a compositional or chronological connection, creating a cohesive whole when brought together.

These recordings are typically packaged in CD or DVD format, usually housed within a rectangular box. The packaging often includes elaborate covers, extensive booklets with high-quality photos, and remastered original album tracks alongside unreleased recordings that didn't make it onto the album.

Additionally, box sets may feature hidden gems that deserved a place on the original album, as well as simple demos showcasing the singer and guitar arrangements.

Live concert recordings from around the time of the album release are also commonly included. While box sets tend to be quite expensive, often priced at £50 or more, they make impressive additions to CD racks and bookcases.

Classic rock bands often cater to a specific demographic with their box sets. These collections tend to attract affluent, young-at-heart individuals who are passionate about collecting and have some disposable income to spare.

Typically, they are older men with greying hair and a nostalgic fondness for the golden era of 1970s prog rock. However, I certainly don't fit into this stereotype.

I'm far too thrifty to splurge all my money on box sets, although there may be a rumour or two about me owning a Jethro Tull box set.

Each Tull album, up to and including *Broadsword And The*

Beast, boasts an extensive box set filled with every conceivable associated recording. These sets come complete with lavishly illustrated booklets brimming with trivia you never knew you needed until you read it.

Steven Wilson, the founder member of the nineties prog rock band Porcupine Tree, is a polymath known for his roles as guitarist, vocalist, and writer.

He's also the mastermind behind the Tull box sets, serving as producer, remixer, remasterer, and rearranger.

When you listen to the box sets, you first hear the original tracks followed by Steven's remasters, allowing you to spot the differences. He might retune a snare drum, enhance a vocal line, or amplify a guitar, among other adjustments in the remix.

In the remastered version of *A Passion Play*, he even reintroduced a couple of lyric lines that Ian had previously dismissed. With his extensive work on the old, remastered albums, Steven Wilson could now be considered a retrospective honorary member of Jethro Tull from the seventies and early eighties.

From Tull's extensive collection of hidden gem tracks associated with box sets, I have several options for this chapter.

One contender is "Part Of The Machine", featured in the *20 Years Of Jethro Tull* box set in 1988 and later included in some editions of *Crest Of A Knave*.

This track embodies Tull's signature style, blending acoustic and rock elements with light and shade, and a fusion of metal and folk influences. Recorded in 1988, it could have easily been an additional track on the *Rock Island* album. However, its similarity to the title track "Rock Island" may explain why it found its place elsewhere instead.

My chosen track is "Jack-A-Lynn", and the journey begins to uncover its different versions across various box sets and compilations.

I must confess, the heartfelt romantic lyrics and Ian's sincere vocals make this song truly special. The name "Jack-A-Lynn" is derived from Ian's wife Shona's middle name, Jacqueline, underscoring the song's theme of longing for loved ones while on the road as a rock star.

For us ordinary folks, being away from our spouse might prompt a slightly sentimental text message, not necessarily inspire one of the greatest love songs of all time (although that might be a slight exaggeration).

"Jack-A-Lynn" version (1) is featured on the box set for *Heavy Horses* CD1, and it's unmistakably a Steven Wilson remix. This rendition is acoustic, featuring sensitive double-tracked vocals accompanied by added piano and organ swells, lasting about four minutes.

Recorded in October 1977, it seemed to have been somewhat overlooked afterwards, perhaps because its overtly romantic lyrics hit a bit too close to home for Ian as a writer, who typically shied away from writing about personal feelings.

Interestingly, there's no flute in this version. The subsequent three versions are all part of the *Broadsword And The Beast* box set from 2023.

"Jack-A-Lynn" (2) is another acoustic rendition. It was recorded in January 1982, four years after the original. It closely resembles the previous version until around the 2:30 mark, where the vocals take on a more impassioned tone.

Interestingly, it was recorded slightly after version (3), and once again, there's no flute in this rendition.

"Jack-A-Lynn" (3) is perhaps the most well-known version of the song. It begins gently and gradually builds up to a loud and raucous climax, featuring a brilliant acoustic/rock fusion that epitomises Tull's signature style.

Martin's guitar work and Gerry Conway's driving drums propel the song forward with intensity. Ian's impassioned vocal delivery adds to the song's power, although it might leave you with a sore throat just listening to it.

Recorded in December 1981, this version remained in the shadows for a few years before being released. And once again, there's no flute in this rendition.

"Jack-A-Lynn" (4) is labelled as a demo version and surprisingly features some flute! It bears similarities to version (3) but lacks the crunchy guitar riff in the rockier section towards the end, resulting in a less intense vibe overall.

Martin delivers a Mark Knopfler-esque guitar solo during the outro, which adds a nice touch but feels somewhat out of place in the context of the track.

"Jack-A-Lynn" (3) was ultimately included in the *20 Years*

Of Jethro Tull box set, specifically on album three, *Flawed Gems And Dusted Down.*

Unlike the earlier iteration (3) found in the *Broadsword And The Beast* box set, this 1988 release had not undergone a remix by Steven Wilson. So, perhaps this version could be dubbed "Jack-A-Lynn" (2.9). If you're following along, the tale isn't quite over yet.

"Jack-A-Lynn" (5) originates from the 25th Anniversary box set in 1992, featured on *The Beacon Bottom Tapes* CD3. It begins like the other renditions, with an acoustic introduction, showcasing Ian's post-1984 singing style.

There's a bit more flute in this version, and during the heavy section toward the end, there are some delightful flute moments that echo Ian's vocal lines. And just when you think it is safe to go back outside, there's more...

"Jack-A-Lynn" (6) was released live as part of a single in 1992, along with "Rocks On the Road", "Bourée", and "Mother Goose".

Additionally, "Jack-A-Lynn" (4), the demo version, was attached to various single releases in 1992.

As for "Jack-A-Lynn" (7), it's associated with live recordings and videos captured during various tours in 1991. A notable performance from Jethro Tull in Istanbul in 1991 is available online for viewing.

It's remarkable how a great song like "Jack-A-Lynn" took about ten years to be publicly released, and then it became available in so many different forms. It can be positively bewildering, even for a superfan like myself. If I've missed any versions out, I apologise to any Tull fans who are even more completist and obsessive than I am.

"Jack-A-Lynn" is universally liked by critics and fans alike, myself included. Acoustic versions (1) and (2) earn 6/10 marks. The demo version (4) also gets 6/10. Any live rendition ((6) and (7)) can have 7/10. The Beacon Bottom version (5) is a solid 8/10, while "Jack-A-Lynn" (3) from 1988, remastered by Steven Wilson for the *Broadsword And The Beast* box set in 2023, gets top marks with 10/10. Then there's "Jack-A-Lynn" (8), my own shower karaoke version, which gets 0/10 and should be avoided at all costs.

26.
Rock Island
Headspace geography

*R*ock Island, Jethro Tull's seventeenth studio album, was recorded in spring 1989 and released in August of that year. It continued in the rock-oriented, radio-friendly direction established with *Crest Of A Knave*. Martin Barre continued to excel with his guitar heroics, and this album featured much more flute compared to its predecessor.

The album includes some interesting tracks. "Kissing Willie" stands out as one of the most trite and embarrassing songs Ian Anderson ever wrote, especially when paired with its Benny Hill-esque vulgar video, which is best avoided. However, it was of its time and perhaps just good bawdy fun.

On the other hand, the album features absolute prog rock epics like "Ears Of Tin" and "The Whaler's Dues".

Following the original "Christmas Song" released as a single in late 1968, the album introduces another Christmas-themed track with great originality and irony, titled "Another Christmas Song" (more on this in chapter 27).

Doane Perry became the permanent drummer, with Peter-John Vettese and Martin Allcock — Dave Pegg's multi-instrumentalist buddy from Fairport Convention — on keyboards. My favourite song on the album, *Rock Island*, is cunningly titled just that: "Rock Island".

There is an actual Rock Island, which is a town of 37,000 people in Illinois, USA. It is located in and around Arsenal Island, which sits in the Mississippi River, about 170 miles south of Chicago.

This settlement is famous for its bridges. Also, Rock Island is a small community within the Ville of Stanstead, Quebec, Canada. There are at least another twenty geographical locations or settlements named Rock Island, mainly in North America.

Probably the largest actual group of real rock islands in the world is the Hawaiian archipelago, which rises over 30,000 feet from the floor of the Pacific Ocean. The ultimate rock island claimed by the UK is Rockall, described as an uninhabited granite islet in the North Atlantic Ocean, only 700 square metres in size.

Closer to home in Northwest Scotland, rock islands with big cliffs and mountains include Arran, Iona, Rhum, Eigg, and Mull. The Isle of Skye is also notable, especially because Ian Anderson owned a small part of it when he lived on the Sraithaird Estate at Kilmarie House during the time of recording.

It is unlikely that Ian Anderson was thinking about any specific places in North America or Scotland when writing the lyrics for the track "Rock Island".

However, he did have his "own little patch of sand" (a lyric from verse three of "Rock Island") as part of his estate on Skye. He lived there throughout the 1980s, and I have always thought there is a hint that his home island location influenced the song.

Skye is certainly rocky, with jagged cliffs, and the even more jagged Cuillin mountain range dominates all viewpoints. Having been to Skye, I cannot help but think of this fantastic rocky wonderland when I hear "Rock Island".

Now it's time to analyse the lyrics, a task I approach with the usual extent of caution. The subjects in the song all seem to have issues, but as long as they end up on the "Rock Island", everything will be okay. In verse three, the lyrics state, "and just as you are drowning, the tide goes down and you are back on your rock island".

It is surely a metaphor for a safe personal headspace where all is well, and no one can reach you. This could manifest physically as your bedroom with a closed door, the box room with sacred and scattered Jethro Tull memorabilia (where I live most of the time), a second home by the sea, or, if you are a millionaire rock star, your own rock island.

I love the line "with your own little patch of sand" as a source of comfort, wellness, happiness, and safety. We can all have our own "Rock Island"; it just might not be quite as big as yours, Ian!

As with many other songs I've covered in this book, it's the riff, melody, rhythm, and musical ensemble playing that really captivate me.

"Rock Island" is structured in four parts. It begins with singing interwoven with replies from guitar and flute. Then, both instruments solo at a rapid pace, followed by more singing with additional flute and guitar weaving.

The track culminates in a fantastic outro featuring guitar and flute stabbing lines, along with a mammoth up-and-down bass line from Dave. Somehow, the track sounds big, rocky, and well-rounded with a few jagged edges — just like your typical rock island.

While "Rock Island" might not make my top ten Tull tracks, it definitely sits comfortably in the top eleven. I love the music, and on an intellectual day, I even claim to understand the lyrics, which I hope I've (more or less) correctly interpreted. It's a rock solid 7/10 for me.

27.
Another Christmas Song
Always time for another and another

Jethro Tull recorded three songs with "Christmas" in the title, along with several others thematically linked to the festive period. All of these were either re-released or newly released on *The Jethro Tull Christmas Album* in 2003.

In late 1968, the aptly named "Christmas Song" was released as the B-side to the "Love Story" single. The lyrics urge listeners not to overindulge during the festive season and to remember that "the Christmas spirit is not what you drink".

At the end of the song, Ian adds, "Hey Santa, pass us that bottle, will ya?" This expected counterbalance punch line is typical of Ian's early songwriting style.

While it could be alcohol in the bottle, I'd prefer to think of it as a remedy for the overindulgence leading up to Christmas. It seems like Santa showed up just in time with the medicine.

The idea that these are some of the most ironic spoken lyrics in the Jethro Tull songbook is hard to deny. Tull definitely does irony, and they do it well! This is a great fun song where you can have it both ways: start off a "goody-goody" and then end up rebellious rock 'n' roll. It's classic Ian Anderson with his signature two-way lyrics.

Musically, "Christmas Song" features Ian on mandolin, tin whistle, and vocals, with string arrangements by David Palmer.

For the Christmas album version, the arrangement was expanded to include extra mandolin from Dave Pegg, drumming from Ian's son James Duncan, and contributions from Martin and Andy on their usual instruments.

"Ring Out, Solstice Bells" features on *Songs From The Wood*. The lyrics celebrate the solstice as a time of fun and frolic for druids and maidens who can "dance in 7 time".

Christmas is referenced with "join together beneath the mistletoe", and the solstice tubular bells, reminiscent of sleigh bells, dominate the track's outro.

The reference to "7 time" in the lyrics probably alludes to the song's 7/4 time signature, which Chrysalis, the record company, found problematic because it was difficult to dance to and tap your feet along with.

Consequently, for the single release, the track was remade with the help of producer Mike Batt, of Womble fame, in a 4/4 time signature to appeal to the lucrative Christmas toe-tapping market.

However, this version was never released, as 4/4 proved too straightforward for late seventies Tull, and the song remained in 7/4. The band did perform it on *Top Of The Pops* approaching Christmas, filling in at short notice for Rod Stewart.

The single reached number 28 on the singles chart in late 1976 before quickly fading away. The original version and the version on the Christmas album are very similar.

My favourite among the three Tull songs with Christmas in the title is "Another Christmas Song", originally featured on *Rock Island*. I adore the lyrics, which convey the idea that despite the chaos in the world, the old man gathers his children for Christmas, evoking a sense of family and belonging.

Another line I particularly love is "everyone is from somewhere, even though you have never been there", suggesting that while we may not know everyone personally, our shared values unite us, making life and Christmas inclusive for all.

Of course, it's possible that I'm reading too much into it, and it's simply another Christmas song. But to me, it surpasses the verbal creativity of Slade, Wizzard, and Bing Crosby. These lyrics are my favourite among all festive songs.

Musically, both the *Rock Island* and Christmas album

versions are similar. Dave Pegg returns on the second version on bass, while Ian spectacularly plays drums on the first version.

Christmas, as a whole, is a delightful time of year, earning a solid 6/10 from me. But a Jethro Tull Christmas elevates the experience. "Christmas Song" earns a 6/10 due to its punch line.

"Ring Out, Solstice Bells" naturally receives a 7/10 because it retained its original 7/4 time signature.

"Another Christmas Song" earns an 8/10 for its profoundly heartwarming lyrics, proving that even if it was just another Christmas song, it stands out.

28.
Rocks On The Road
Rock star; hard life

I can't even begin to imagine what it's like to be a touring musician, especially for over fifty years. The closest I've come is accompanying school children on geography field trips during my days as a teacher.

Those trips lasted just a week, we stayed put, and there were certainly no sound checks involved. I've also done some youth hostel tours around Scotland, moving every couple of days, climbing mountains.

The closest I've come to the stereotypical tour experience of sex, drugs, and rock 'n' roll was hiking up Ben Macdui in the Cairngorms with a girl from London whom I had met at the hostel.

She was worried about leaving her oven on at home before coming to Scotland, so romance wasn't exactly on her mind (I never did find out if she had left the oven on).

As it was the early nineties, the most rock 'n' roll thing we did was listen to my tape of *Catfish Rising* in the car.

Ian and Martin, in particular, must have spent a good portion of their lives on the road, constantly travelling between gigs and staying in hotels.

Up until the end of 2022, Tull had performed live 3207 times, Ian Anderson had done 1038 shows, and Martin Barre, solo, had performed 614 times, totalling 4859 performances between them.

That's an enormous amount of time away from home, with hardly any time to change your socks.

By all accounts, Jethro Tull were always a well-behaved band on the road. There were no tales of televisions being hurled out of hotel windows, no Harley Davidsons being ridden down hotel corridors, or any x-rated escapades with fish, as some Led Zeppelin stories would have you believe.

If I pretend that I once wrote to Ian asking him about life on the road, I'll assume that in his reply, he told me he would address my question with the next Tull album, their eighteenth, *Catfish Rising*: "Rocks On The Road" would paint a picture of a life on tour that wasn't all glitz and glamour.

Catfish Rising hit the shelves in September 1991 after being recorded earlier that spring. It continued the hard rock streak of the two preceding albums, featuring tracks like "Doctor To My Disease" and "This Is Not Love".

However, it also showcased folk and blues influences with songs such as "A Tall Thin Girl" and "Sleeping With The Dog". The album boasted a line-up that included Ian and Martin, along with three keyboard players: Andy Giddings, Foss Peterson, and John "Rabbit" Bundrick.

Additionally, there were two drummers, primarily Doane, and Scott Hunter, with the latter being uncredited on "Loving You Tonight".

Notably, there was a father-son bass duo featuring Dave and his son Matthew, who stepped in for his dad during three tracks while Dave was occupied with Fairport Convention (or possibly washing his non-existent hair).

For the subsequent tour, Martin Allcock returned to handle keyboards, despite not having contributed to the album's recording. If there are any inaccuracies here, blame it on Ian's penchant for collaborating with too many musicians in too short a timeframe for me to keep track of!

"Rocks On The Road" is just such a cool song. I adore the lyrics, particularly how "a little light music can chase it all away". It paints a picture of the unglamorous life of a rock star on tour.

Then again, maybe Ian was referring to someone else, like a travelling salesman? The lyrics touch on various issues encountered on the road, from police fights outside hotels to noisy plumbing, overloaded mini bars, and hefty phone bills, all of which can "spoil my day".

These lyrics resonate with me because life on the road can easily mirror life's everyday challenges, where countless little things can pile up and dampen spirits — not just for rock stars, but for all of us.

It's a thoroughly sombre song until the line "how about a little light music to chase it all away?" The mention of the BBC Light Programme, the precursor to BBC Radio 2, suggests that Ian may have been recommending smooth, classic pop tunes of the day to lift spirits.

Something gentle like Dionne Warwick's "Do You Know The Way To San Jose", a smooth classic, could do the trick and aid relaxation. It's funny how tastes evolve over time. I used to dislike that song, but now I appreciate Dionne, Tull, Neil Young, Holst, Elgar, and others. Where did I go wrong/right?

Musically, "Rocks On The Road" maintains a mid-paced tempo with a bluesy vibe, featuring interwoven acoustic and electric guitars, along with flute melodies, complemented by some intricate bass lines courtesy of substitute family member, Mathew Pegg.

There's a subtle touch of piano and synthesised string keyboard, presumably played by Ian, as no other keyboardist is credited for this track.

Over the years, "Rocks On The Road" has made sporadic appearances in live performances. Notably, during the 1992 Little Light Music tour, Ian, Martin, Dave, and Dave Mattocks on drums performed the song, with Dave M stepping in during a leave of absence from Fairport Convention. It's interesting how Fairport and Tull seemed interchangeable in terms of personnel at that time.

"Rocks On The Road" is widely regarded by fans, critics, and myself as the standout track on *Catfish Rising*. It easily earns a 7/10 rating, sharing the top spot with "Rock Island" as one of the best Tull tracks with "Rock" in the title.

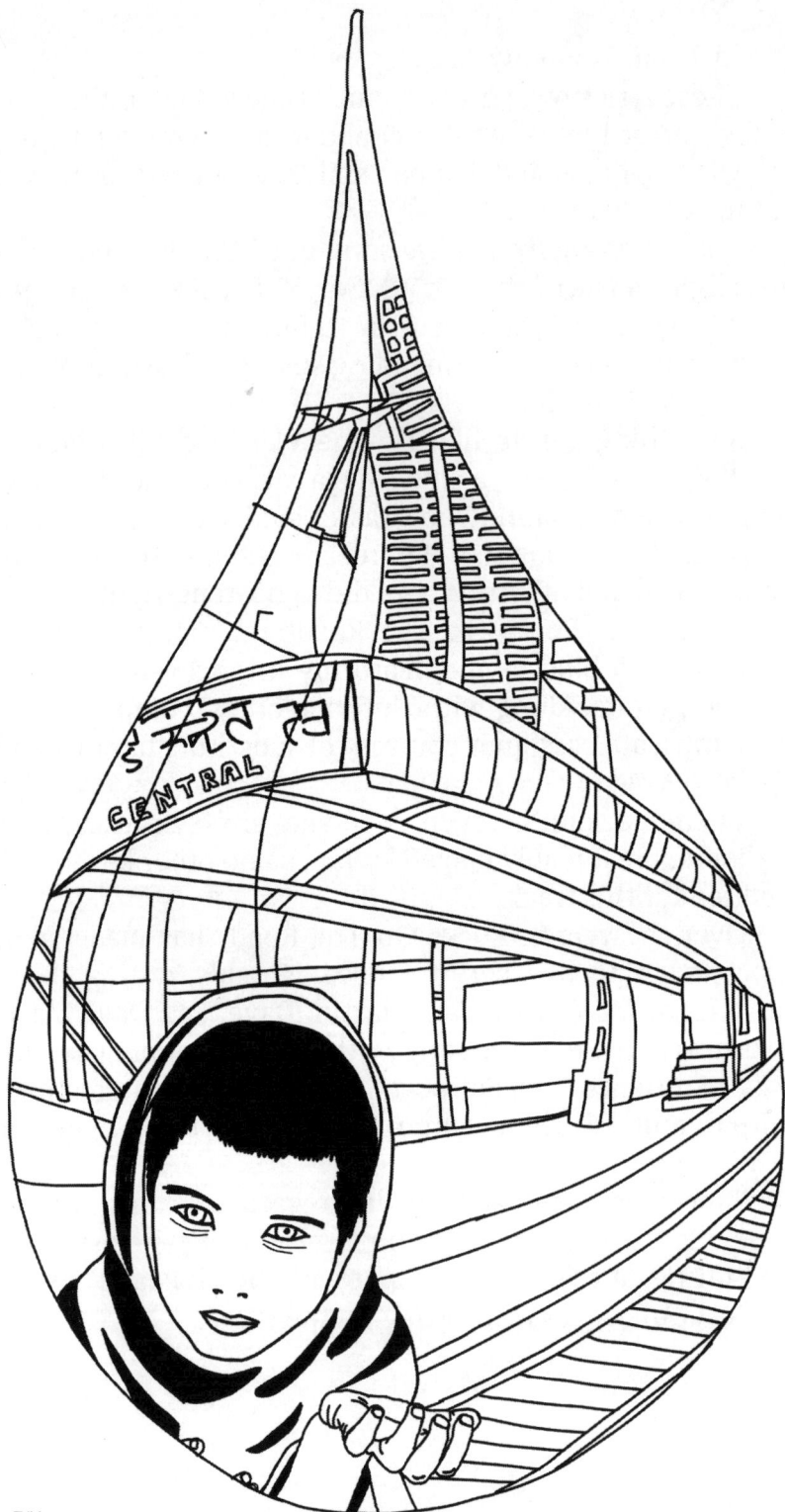

© Elaine Tribley

140

29.
Beside Myself
Just sad, sad, sad and serious

A lot happened in the world of Jethro Tull between 1991, when *Catfish Rising* was released, and 1995, with the arrival of *Roots To Branches*.

Various tours took place, including the 25th anniversary tour, which extended well into 1994, effectively becoming the 26th anniversary tour. Additionally, several compilation albums celebrating Tull's silver jubilee were released, along with the live album, *A Little Light Music*.

During this period, Dave Pegg became increasingly semi-detached from the band, finding it difficult to balance his commitments to Jethro Tull with his responsibilities in Fairport Convention, where he was organising, directing, playing, and drinking.

Consequently, for *Roots To Branches*, Dave only played on three tracks. The remaining tracks featured American Steve Bailey, an academic bass guitar teacher and all-around virtuoso nice bloke. By this time, Andy Giddings had become the permanent keyboard player for Tull.

Perhaps the biggest change during this period concerned Ian Anderson's approach to playing the flute and the types of flutes he chose.

For about twenty-five years, starting in 1968, Anderson played the flute in a breathy, jazzy, bluesy style that became his trademark.

However, in 1993, his daughter, also a flute player, allegedly told him that his fingering was incorrect. This prompted him to learn the flute properly. A more likely story is that, on a whim in India, he decided to relearn the flute and had some fingering charts faxed over from England. These charts helped him correct his technique, particularly his embouchure, which involves proper breathing into the flute.

As a result, Anderson could now play classical flute with a sound comparable to that of James Galway on a very good day. This transition also led him to explore bamboo and wooden flutes, which added an Indian world music sound to both his solo album *Divinities: Twelve Dances With God* and *Roots To Branches*.

Bamboo and wooden flutes, ancient predecessors to modern metallic ones, produce a soft, mellow, and muffled sound, distinct from the bright, sharp tones of nickel, silver, or gold flutes.

On the track "In The Grip Of Stronger Stuff" from Divinities, which some believe reflects on Dave Pegg's drinking habits, Anderson starts with a metal flute. At 1:14, a bamboo flute joins in, and the two flutes alternate until this great little track ends at 2:43.

By this time, Ian's flute playing had reached another level, although he could still revert to his breathy, jazzy style when needed.

Consequently, *Catfish Rising* began to feel like ancient history compared to the virtuoso flute performances, intricate musical motifs, and deep, meaningful lyrics present on *Roots To Branches*.

This album marked a return to a more serious tone for Jethro Tull, and it remains an album I play for enjoyment, not just for reference. For me, "Beside Myself" is the standout track on the album.

Lyrically, this album delves into heavy themes. Gone are the world-weary, self-indulgent lyrics of "Rocks On The Road" from *Catfish Rising*. Instead, it tackles issues like poverty and the harsh realities children face in Bombay.

This might be the saddest song Ian has ever written — until two tracks later on the album, with "At Last, Forever", which contemplates death. These intense, observational songs permeate the album, leading fans and critics alike to hail it as a return to the essence of Jethro Tull, in stark contrast to the playfulness of *Catfish Rising*.

Instrumentally, the song starts with an acoustic guitar that reminds me of "My God" from *Aqualung*. It then transitions to a keyboard lead with stabbing guitar chords and showcases Ian's refined flute fingering.

The instrumental break really rocks, with perfect playing that balances soft and loud, light and heavy elements. Ian's mature voice is perfect for this song; twenty years earlier, his vocals would have been too harsh and lacked the sensitivity needed for a song like this.

It's clear I have a strong appreciation for this song. This is classic Tull in all its melancholic finery. It gets a solid 9.5/10 from me.

© Bekah Elliott

30.
Hot Mango Flush/
Mango Surprise
Weird or wot?

By 1999, Andy Giddings was firmly established as Ian's go-to virtuoso keyboard player for Jethro Tull. Despite having no formal musical training and initially playing by ear, by the time he joined Tull, there seemed to be nothing he couldn't do musically. He even seemed to enjoy playing the piano accordion.

The other new member was Jonathan Noyce, an exceptional bass guitarist who took over from Dave Pegg in 1995 when Pegg returned to his first love, Fairport Convention.

Born in 1971, Jonathan was likely conceived while his parents were listening to *Benefit* and was subsequently influenced by the new Tull record, *Aqualung*, released in 1971 during his early infancy.

That is, at least, the myth behind his joining Tull. While Tull mythology is rich with such rumours and legends, I cannot guarantee the veracity of these statements.

After that moment of levity, now to the serious business of *J-Tull Dot Com*, my least favourite Tull album title.

Recorded early in 1999 and released in August 1999, the title strikes me as a crude attempt at trendy modernity that quickly became outdated. In today's world, where the Internet is ubiquitous, the title hasn't aged well.

However, it did spawn a great song: "Dot.Com", the best track on the album, featuring the full band and enhanced by Najma Akhtar on backing vocals. It's definitely worth a 9/10.

The album as a whole is similar in outline to *Roots To Branches*, although perhaps not quite as good. I also enjoy "Wicked Windows", a song about glasses, which I can relate to in my optically challenged old age.

I love the heavy riff in the cat-themed "Hunt By Numbers". Perhaps the most divisive song Tull ever did, along with "The Story Of The Hare Who Lost His Spectacles", is "Hot Mango Flush/Mango Surprise".

I will treat these two seemingly separate songs as one. Although they are three tracks apart on the album, "Mango Surprise" is essentially just the outro to "Hot Mango Flush". I find these songs amazing — whether that's amazingly good or bad, I'm never quite sure — but they could easily be the most interesting tracks on the album.

They may be untypical of Tull, but the band being experimental, diverse, and different is what I and many others love about Tull. You never quite know what to expect.

Compared to "The Story Of The Hare Who Lost His Spectacles", "Hot Mango Flush/Mango Surprise" feels positively conservative.

The song was co-written: Martin composed the music and Ian penned the lyrics. Musically, it is led by Martin's guitar, with flute and keyboard flourishes. At 1:35, there's a great acoustic guitar solo, perhaps the highlight of the track. In the last thirty seconds, Martin also contributes further acoustic meanderings, which enhance the song even more.

The lyrics to "Hot Mango Flush" offer an observation of life in the Caribbean, which Ian and Martin had recently visited. The delivery is half-spoken, almost rap-like, which is quite unusual for Tull.

Although the meaning of the words may be obscure, the voice acts as an instrument to enhance the rhythm, which I find really appealing. Ian Anderson as a pseudo-rapper — who would have ever believed it?

Even better, I love the sparseness, trilling flute, and wonderfully funky percussion from Doane on "Mango Surprise", which has no formal lyrics apart from Ian repeating "hot mango flush".

Despite extensive searching online, trawling through books

and magazines, and interviewing all my Tull-oriented friends, I can't find anyone who has a good word to say about "Hot Mango Flush/Mango Surprise".

However, listening to it now as I write, it's not bad and it's so cool for Tull to create a track like this, what with it being so atypical.

Of course, because this is Jethro Tull we're talking about, it's not atypical at all, but rather the band at their experimental best, trying something different.

Therefore, from me, "Hot Mango Flush" gets a 7/10 and "Mango Surprise" gets an 8/10, which averages out to 8/10 overall. I could never do arithmetic at school.

© Bekah Elliott

31.
First Snow on Brooklyn
When love goes wrong, again

Christmas is a multifaceted event encompassing religious, cultural, social, family, and commercial aspects that most people generally love to celebrate.

The word "Christmas" originates from "Christian Mass", the religious service held on 25th December. This date is linked to the winter solstice on 21st December, marking a time of spiritual and physical renewal as spring slowly approaches.

On the other hand, Christmas often represents a period of excessive consumerism, gluttony, being in the grip of stronger stuff (alcohol), and family conflicts.

More poignantly, as I write in December 2023, it seems to be a time when war, death, and destruction persist. This juxtaposition of joy and sorrow makes the season bittersweet and reflective.

Still though, Christmas can also serve as a time for family and friends to come together in warmth and tenderness. It offers a chance for people of all faiths to unite in positive harmony, even if just for a few days.

In the realm of pop music, Christmas songs are a perennial tradition. Everyone from Bing Crosby to Slade to Band Aid, even iconic acts like U2, Queen, The Eagles, and Bruce Springsteen, have embraced it.

The question arises: does releasing a Christmas song compromise artistic integrity, or is it simply an act of joining in with the festive fun? If even the likes of Bruce Springsteen can do it, perhaps it's acceptable?

Charity Christmas records, like those of Band Aid, certainly carry a noble purpose. These songs, stored away in vaults and resurrected annually by radio stations, DJs, and retailers, become synonymous with the holiday season.

Slade's "Merry Christmas Everybody" famously recorded in sweltering July heat, exemplifies the commercial foresight behind planning for Christmas well in advance. With the exception of charity records, it's the time for Christmas capitalists to capitalise on the festive spirit.

However, for established artists with decades of musical prowess, why not craft a Christmas album of artistic merit? Whether featuring original compositions, revamped classics, or traditional carols, such albums can offer profound yet lighthearted insights.

This is precisely what Jethro Tull did in 2003, releasing their Christmas album in September, strategically timed for the extended pre-Christmas sales season.

Ian Anderson has always had a soft spot for Christmas. He's known for his seasonal church performances across England, where both as a solo artist and now with the modern Tull, he delivers an eclectic set, often in support of church charities.

The Christmas album draws inspiration from various sources, including the winter solstice, wintry weather, and even Bach, alongside more traditional seasonal themes found in Tull's three Christmas songs: "Christmas Song", "Ring Out, Solstice Bells", and "Another Christmas Song".

While it's unclear as to how Bach's "Bourrée" fits into a Christmas album, it's presented as an updated version that's enjoyable to listen to.

On a related note, unlike the lack of Christmas snow in the UK, New York often experiences snowfall, setting the stage for "First Snow On Brooklyn", my personal favourite track on the album.

I don't just enjoy this song; I absolutely adore it. It holds a place in my top five favourite Tull tracks, despite its sombre lyrics.

Yes, the lyrics indeed evoke a sense of sadness as they depict two lovers unable to be together on Christmas night, leaving behind only "crunchy footprints in the snow" where one had looked up to "the cosy window frame" of the other.

Is it a break-up song? Or, considering the lyric "you don't see me in the shadows from your cosy window frame", perhaps a modern-day Romeo and Juliet tale? (albeit not a Dire Straits track).

Regardless, it's a poignant narrative of lovers separated during the holiday season. While it may never top the charts like festive classics with Santa, turkey, or reindeer, it deeply resonates with listeners, almost bringing me to tears each time I hear it. It's another Tull song without quite the happy ending... again!

The lush strings, courtesy of The Sturcz String Quartet, combined with Ian's flute, create an immersive experience in this truly remarkable song. The melody is simply enchanting.

Am I just a sentimental softie? Perhaps, but this song has that effect on me. With a contemporary and trendy artist singing it, I believe it could still become a future Christmas hit. Maybe Justin Bieber?

I have no choice but to award this song a 10/10, or possibly even an 11/10. I've always been a bit extravagant with numbers.

32.
In Brief Visitation
Nineteen years later

Between their twenty-first and twenty-second studio albums, a lot happened in the world of Jethro Tull. Firstly, nineteen years had elapsed, which is quite remarkable considering the band's prolific output in the 1970s when they released an album annually.

However, during this period, the band remained active with live performances from 2003 to 2011.

Andy Giddings and Jonathan Noyce departed, and in 2007, they were replaced by John O'Hara on keyboards and Dave Goodier on bass. Yet, the most sombre event occurred in 2011 when the band disbanded, leaving Doane Perry, after twenty-seven years, and Martin Barre, after an incredible forty-two years, out in the cold.

Ian desired to collaborate with different musicians under his own name. Since then, Martin has gone it alone and is currently touring the Tull repertoire with his own band, experiencing considerable success with it.

Up until 2011, Ian's solo albums deviated from the typical Tull sound. *Walk Into Light* (1983), with assistance from Peter-John Vitesse, delved into electronic territory and lacked guitar presence. *Divinities: Twelve Dances With God* (1995) was a classical endeavour reminiscent of James Galway, showcasing Ian's new flute technique.

Meanwhile, *The Secret Language Of Birds* (2000) and *Rupi's Dance* (2003) adopted an acoustic, singer-songwriter approach. While each album featured noteworthy songs, they felt more like Ian's solo ventures rather than offerings from Jethro Tull.

This brings us to *Thick As A Brick 2* (2012), released by the Ian Anderson Band rather than Jethro Tull. The line-up consisted of Ian, John, David, guitarist Florian Opahle, and Scott Hammond on drums, with additional studio assistance from wind player Peter Judge and vocalist Ryan O'Donnel, who also toured with the band to aid Ian in singing and presentation.

Personally, I quite enjoyed the album, with "Kismet In Suburbia" standing out as my favourite track. However, it's worth noting that despite its musical and lyrical resemblance to Tull, *Thick As A Brick 2* wasn't a Tull album, which might seem odd as a sequel to *Thick As A Brick 1*.

Nonetheless, the follow-up live shows featuring both *Thick As A Brick 1* and *Thick As A Brick 2* segments were highly enjoyable for me and many other fans.

Florian showcased his virtuosity on the guitar, although he may not have been a perfect Martin Barre replacement. Additionally, the absence of an "Aqua/Breath" encore was a bold move.

Homo Erraticus, released in 2014, marked Ian's final solo album, featuring some standout tracks. Similar to *Thick As A Brick 1*, the more seasoned Gerald Bostock contributed to the lyrics here.

Nearly wrapping up our historical journey, there's also the *Jethro Tull – The String Quartets* album released in 2017. The debate continues: was it Tull, was it Ian, was it simply a string quartet, and was it any good? I've never quite settled my thoughts on this one.

In 2017, the return of Jethro Tull unfolded as Ian decided it was fitting for his longstanding band to release an album under the Jethro Tull name, acknowledging their dedication, reliability, and years of performing older tracks faithfully.

Thus, *The Zealot Gene* emerged. Yet, for some fans, the absence of Martin Barre posed a challenge. I found myself somewhat in this camp as well. Nevertheless, I welcomed the opportunity to enjoy new music from Ian and Tull.

The album was recorded between 2017 and 2021, a process stretched out by tours and further prolonged by COVID-related interruptions.

The Zealot Gene embodies the quintessential Tull blend of acoustic and electric elements, light and shade, coupled with intellectually engaging lyrics that demand contemplation.

While I've struggled to fully embrace the album overall, certain tracks like "Mrs Tibbets" and "Sad City Sisters" have caught my attention. However, it's track eleven that stands out remarkably for me.

Track eleven is "In Brief Visitation". It deviates from the album's usual tone, which is precisely why I find it so captivating. There's a profound beauty in its arrangement and Ian's delicate vocals, despite the sombre undertone of the lyrics, which depict the fall guy bearing the burden of collective sins.

This track resonates with me deeply, even though I haven't felt as drawn to the rest of the album. The interplay between flute and electric guitar evokes echoes of Ian and Martin, despite the latter's absence.

The remarkably young and talented Joe Parrish makes his Tull recording debut, having replaced Florian Opahle towards the end of *The Zealot Gene's* production.

While "In Brief Visitation" may not crack the top five of all acoustic tracks, it certainly earns an honourable mention, securing a solid number six spot.

While I'd rate *The Zealot Gene* as a whole, a modest 5/10, this particular song shines brightly at a strong 9/10.

Yet, despite my fondness for this standout track, the rest of the album still fails to resonate with me. I'm left pondering why that might be the case. Any insights? All answers on a postcard, please.

156

33.
Ginnungagap
Ragnorok would be devastated

Back in the late nineties, I seem to recall that the million-dollar question on the American version of *Who Wants To Be A Millionaire* was on who won the heavy metal/hard rock Grammy in 1989.

Surprisingly, it wasn't Metallica, but a gentle folk prog rock ensemble from England. This band was renowned for their iconic frontman, a flute player who famously performed standing on one leg.

Unfortunately, the name of this band eludes me at the moment. Fast-forward to 2024, and the equivalent question on *Who Wants To Be A Millionaire* would probably involve a contestant being required to spell out the name of track two on Jethro Tull's 2023 album, *RökFlöte*. The track starts with 'G', but beyond that, you'd need the best of Nordic luck from the Nordic gods.

RökFlöte and its titular track are part of Jethro Tull's Norse mythology-themed album. Norse gods often make appearances In popular culture, as seen in Marvel films with characters like Thor, Loki, and Odin.

The lyrics of *RökFlöte* delve into various deities, both benevolent and malevolent, from Nordic legend and folklore. Detailed sleeve notes accompany the album, providing insight into these mythological figures.

One particularly intriguing character is Ragnarok, who sounds like he could be a rugged, intimidating Norwegian football defender.

However, Ragnarok is actually a concept depicting the end of the world in Norse mythology, as prophesied in the Icelandic poem "Voluspa" from the late 13th century.

The character features in the title of the 2017 film *Thor: Ragnorok*. Then there is the God Of War (Ragnorok) computer game with the song "Blood Upon The Snow" by Bear McCreary and Hozier.

It's about winter and nature's harshness. It would have gone well on *Heavy Horses*, had it been a Tull track.

In *RökFlöte*, Ragnarok signifies Armageddon, but the album also touches on the concept of rebirth with "Ithavoli", the uplifting final track. This narrative parallels the cyclical nature of Norse mythology, where destruction is followed by renewal. The world survives another day and can await the next Jethro Tull Album.

It reminds me of Dr Who mythology (which I am sure Ian will cover on the next Tull album). One might speculate that the Time Wars on Gallifrey, the Doctor's home planet, share similarities with Ragnarok.

Both involve cataclysmic events followed by the possibility of restoration. While there's been no explicit "Doctor Who" reference in any Tull album so far, who knows what Ian Anderson might explore in the future?

Perhaps it's time for a rest and some contemplation. After all, there's never been a hint of a subtle "Doctor Who" nod in any Tull album... until now.

"Ginnungagap" is the second track on side one of the album. It appears to represent both a void, devoid of any life, and a primordial proto-being. One might wonder if this ancient entity would even remember its own name, let alone be able to spell it!

The lyrics delve into complex themes of world creation and divine glorification, offering some clues. However, lines like "folded origami" in verse three add a touch of whimsy, even if their meaning remains elusive to those like me, who are not a Norse god.

For over more than fifty-five years, has any other long-standing band displayed the lyrical diversity that Tull has? While I may grasp about seventy percent of their lyrics, the remaining thirty percent often carry a mysterious quality that occasionally reveals itself in moments of clarity, allowing me to understand them better.

I doubt Bob Dylan would ever write anything quite like this, although Jon Anderson of Yes fame might give it a shot.

The music follows a somewhat predictable pattern, typical of later-day non-acoustic Tull. Flute melodies intertwine with grungy guitar, followed by Ian's vocals, with flute and guitar lines doubling-up afterwards.

There's a notable absence of acoustic elements throughout the album, unfortunately. However, the standout feature is Ian's soft, mature voice, gracefully delivering the song's lyrics with dignity and poise. The single was released in January 2023 along with its own cartoon-style video.

At the time of writing in January 2024, *RökFlöte* is a puzzling album for me. Despite repeated listens, I haven't found a single song that resonates. Even now, as I write these words, I struggle to connect with any of the tracks.

While I wasn't a fan of *The Zealot Gene* overall, there was one standout track ("In Brief Visitation") that I adored — it may even make it into my top ten Tull songs (see the concluding chapter).

As for "Ginnungagap", it only earns a 4/10 from me. *RökFlöte* as a whole would receive a similar rating, perhaps even higher if it incorporated more acoustic elements.

However, if I were to rate the album based solely on its title — a four-syllable, eleven-letter word that only Jethro Tull could release as a single — it would undoubtedly receive a perfect 10/10. Unfortunately, that's not the case.

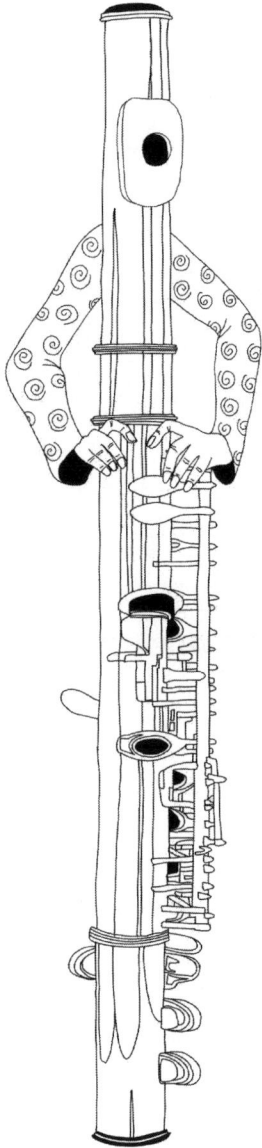

34.
And A Third: Jump Start
Solos that can write 633 words

Before I got started on this chapter, I realised that many classic rock songs feature guitar solos that can make up anywhere between ten percent to over fifty percent of the track.

For example, Jimmy Page's solo in "Stairway To Heaven" by Led Zeppelin takes up just ten percent of the song, while the epic soloing in Lynyrd Skynyrd's "Freebird" occupies a staggering fifty-four percent of the track, lasting almost five minutes of the nine-minute song. This provides ample opportunity for extended head banging, if you're so inclined.

In Jethro Tull's "Aqualung", Martin Barre's solo makes up seventeen percent of the track. This is somewhat unusual for Tull, as their songs often feature a second soloist — Ian Anderson on flute.

For this chapter, I want to cover a Jethro Tull song where both Ian and Martin have solos that collectively take up about thirty-three percent of the song. Let's (jump) start with this idea and see where it takes us.

"Jump Start", track three from *Crest Of A Knave*, is quintessential Jethro Tull. The song begins with an acoustic intro, followed by verses and a chorus, interspersed with flute and guitar interjections.

A flute solo leads into more verses and the chorus, concluding with a guitar solo, all within four minutes and fifty-three seconds.

As a rock blockbuster, it's the second major track after "Steel Monkey" on the album. This song probably contributed to

Jethro Tull's win of the 1989 Grammy for Best Hard Rock/Metal Performance, a surprising and often-discussed achievement covered earlier in this book.

The flute solo is always an iconic hook for Jethro Tull, serving as their unique selling point. Ian Anderson has excelled at these breathy outbursts over the last fifty-five years.

Equally prominent throughout the band's history though, has been the soaring guitar solos from Martin Barre. Both of these elements feature prominently on "Jump Start", so let's examine how the timing plays out.

The track is four minutes and fifty-three seconds long. It features a forty-one-second flute solo midway through and a fifty-three-second guitar solo in the outro. Together, these solos make up thirty-one percent of the entire track.

Since a third is approximately thirty-three percent, I almost have a third of the track covered with these solos.

Finding an exact thirty-three percent solo presence in any Tull track was challenging, akin to finding a flute solo in a Status Quo song. After all, what's two percent among Tullite friends?

The flute solo starts at 2:24, overlaying crunchy guitar chords from Martin Barre, backed up and propelled by Dave Pegg on bass and Gerry Conway on drums, who worked as a session player for this track since Doane Perry was unavailable.

At the end of this sequence, Ian's flute and Martin's guitar double-up. Despite the track's hard rock energy, the soloing has a definite Celtic feel.

The guitar solo starts at 4:03, with Martin Barre delivering a feedback-driven, bouncy, and fluid performance reminiscent of Billy Gibbons from ZZ Top. This solo is further enhanced by vocal whoops and hollers on every fourth beat.

Famously, when this was played live in subsequent years, the backstage roadies would come out with inflatable guitars, head-banging through Martin's heavy metal monster solo.

This playful act also perhaps contributed towards the band's infamous Grammy win; Metallica didn't bring their roadies out for "Enter Sandman". However, their *Black Album*, which features "Enter Sandman", deservedly won the heavy metal Grammy in 1992. Jethro Tull didn't release a studio album that year, so there was no competition.

While it might feel like cheating to give an overall mark for "Jump Start", I can't help but sneak it an 8/10. However, focusing on the "and a third" chunk of the track — the solos — I believe a 9/10 is well-deserved for both Ian's flute and Martin's guitar.

Conclusion
And in the end

In 2024, Ian Anderson was seventy-six years old, approaching seventy-seven. He has been playing the flute and singing with Jethro Tull and his solo bands since 1968, spanning an impressive fifty-five years.

This encompasses 3,267 Tull concerts and 1,038 solo gigs through the end of 2023, totalling 4,305 performances.

On average, each performance lasts about two hours, amounting to 8,810 hours (or 367 days — just over a year of continuous live performing). In comparison, the cumulative live performance hours for footballers over their careers would be considerably less.

Perhaps only a fifty-five-year career theatre actor would have as many live contact hours with an audience.

In the rock star world, if we conservatively estimate a minimum of twenty hours of recording time per album (twenty-three albums in total), that's another four hundred and sixty hours.

Additionally, countless more hours are spent on promotion, interviews, and travelling. This results in a phenomenal amount of time dedicated to being a public performing rock star and recording artist.

Given that much of this work involves singing, talking, and playing the flute, it's no wonder Ian Anderson might feel tired and occasionally experience vocal issues!

Aged rock stars of a similar vintage have also put in countless hours, although they don't have the added challenge of playing the flute.

Mick Jagger, for example, has the face of an older person (sorry Mick, but you do), yet the body of a twenty-year-old and a singing voice sharp enough to cut glass.

Van Morrison, still as grumpy as ever, has a voice that has thickened and matured with age. Bruce Dickinson from Iron Maiden can still deliver powerful vocals, as can Paul Rodgers.

On the other hand, some veteran rockers are beginning to

show signs of vocal strain. While it's generally easier for ageing instrumentalists to continue performing — since they can simply stand or sit with their instrument — it's the singers who often bear the brunt of criticism.

Paul McCartney, for example, can't hit the high notes as he once could, but he still plays a mean bass, guitar, and piano.

At Glastonbury in 2022, he struggled with the high notes on "Maybe I'm Amazed". Similarly, Ian Gillan from Deep Purple, Rob Halford from Judas Priest, and Brian Johnson from AC/DC sometimes find the high notes challenging.

However, why should any of these artists retire? They can still put on a great show, loved by fans, by adapting their singing to lower registers and modifying the set list. Retirement is a long time, and life even longer, so why stop performing when the fans still adore them, and a nice cup of hot chocolate awaits at the end of the show?

In 2024, Ian's struggles with his vocals, particularly during live performances, are well-documented due to his history of throat problems. This topic often sparks discussions among fans on social media, with opinions divided.

Personally, I've developed a theory: Ian would perhaps be a more robust vocalist if he didn't also play the flute, whistle, harmonica, and various saxophones, both in the past and occasionally now. Being a multi-tasking heavy breather, constantly switching between singing and flute playing, likely takes its toll.

While Mick, Van, Bruce, and Paul focus solely on vocals, Ian's unique blend of singing and flute-playing is unparalleled in rock music. The only comparable figure, Thijs van Leer from Focus, didn't sing much besides some falsetto warbling on "Hocus Pocus".

Interestingly, contemporary artist Lizzo, despite being stylistically different from Ian and Tull, excels at both flute-playing and singing. It'll be intriguing to see how her vocal performance evolves over the years.

In recent years, Ian has received assistance on vocals. Ryan O'Donnell took on a significant singing role during the Thick As A Brick tours in 2012-13, allowing Ian to focus more on flute playing.

Bassist Dave Goodier also lends his vocal talents when needed. However, the most remarkable support came from Joe Parrish as guitarist and singer, and currently in 2024, from brand new boy, guitarist and singer Jack Clark.

Additionally, there's the enthusiastic participation of superfan Marc Almond, formerly of Soft Cell, who often joins Ian and Tull for their church Christmas shows, where he always gives "Locomotive Breath" a good seeing-to.

Ian is acutely aware of his vocal limitations. He contends that while he may have been a better singer in the past, his proficiency as a flute player has improved over time, presenting a trade-off.

Additionally, Ian has disclosed that he experiences the early stages of chronic obstructive pulmonary disease, which can directly impact breathing and potentially lead to asthma. He manages this condition with medication. With his characteristic sense of humour, he jests that the rest of his body is in full working order!

In 2024, Ian and Jethro Tull can still deliver a remarkable performance, albeit different from what audiences experienced in 1974 or even 1984. As for the future, I'll delve into that later on.

In the book, I outlined the general reasons for selecting the 33 1/3 songs in the introduction. It's crucial to stress that these choices were made to highlight tracks of specific interest that can spark discussions and exploration. They don't necessarily represent my all-time 33 1/3 favourites.

In fact, a couple of them are rather lacklustre and were included to illustrate particular points about Tull's trajectory at the time.

There are songs I wish I could have included but didn't make the cut. For instance, "Wondering Aloud" couldn't be chosen since I had already selected the two most obvious tracks from *Aqualung*: the title track and "Locomotive Breath".

Similarly, I would have loved to include "Budapest" from *Crest Of A Knave*, as it exemplifies the lengthy, prog rock, epic style, but I had already chosen "Steel Monkey" from that album to demonstrate that Tull could veer towards a metal sound.

Among the more eccentric and obscure tracks, "A Small

Cigar", featured on the remastered versions of the *Too Old To Rock 'n' Roll: Too Young To Die* album, could have been a fun addition.

It has become customary for books of this kind, which analyse something through a specific numerical lens, such as 33 1/3, to include some form of best-of list(s).

I won't be doing that; it feels too clichéd and predictable... On the other hand, perhaps I'll indulge just a bit, and then maybe a bit more, purely for the sake of sparking some lively debate. After all, who doesn't enjoy arguing over the merits of inclusion in a best-of list?

So, here's the definitive countdown list for all 33 tracks, each with its own Strictly Come Tull mark. If there's more than one version, I've taken the average or median mark — essentially, the one in the middle. I've also fixed some of the questionable maths behind certain marks.

I've excluded the third of a song, "Jump Start". In ascending order, it goes something like this:

2/10	Apogee
4/10	Gunnungagap
6.5/10	A Song For Jeffrey
7/10	Too Old To Rock 'n' Roll: Too Young To Die Clasp Rock Island Rocks On The Road
7.5/10	Under Wraps With You There To Help Me Hot Mango Flush Aqualung

8/10	Skating Away On The Thin Ice Of a New Day
	And the Mouse Police Never Sleeps...
	The Pine Marten's Jig
	Another Christmas Song
	Pibroch (Cap In Hand)
	Weathercock

8.5/10	The Story Of The Hare Who Lost His Spectacles

9/10	Back To The Family
	Dharma For One
	Locomotive Breath
	Baker St Muse
	Steel Monkey
	In Brief Visitation

9.5/10	Thick As A Brick
	Beside Myself

The following tracks all received a stellar 10/10 rating. Here they all are, listed in ascending order of my current favourites:

> Jack-A-Lynn
> Living In The Past
> Fire At Midnight
> First Snow On Brooklyn
> Bourée
> Dun Ringill
> Life Is A Long Song

As I near the conclusion of this book, I find myself pleasantly surprised by the evolution of my ratings throughout the writing process. It's gratifying to see that even recent Tull tracks, like "In Brief Visitation" from 2022, have earned high scores.

The top three choices on my list hold special significance for me, each with its own unique charm.

"Bourée" remains a perennial favourite, its cool vibe enduring over the years.

"Dun Ringill" transports me to the ethereal landscapes of Scotland, capturing the essence of Celtic beauty.

"Life Is A Long Song" holds a special place as my introduction to Jethro Tull, its beauty, finesse, and poetic lyrics leaving a lasting impression. It also happens to make for a fitting title for a book about Jethro Tull (at least, I hope so).

Interestingly, none of the top seven songs are outright rockers; they lean more towards acoustic arrangements with sensitive lyrics.

Even "Jack-A-Lynn", at its best, is devoid of flute. However, when it comes to in-your-face rock anthems, "Steel Monkey" takes the crown, despite the iconic status of "Aqualung".

"Bourée" naturally stands out as the best instrumental, with J.S. Bach making a notable contribution that many would agree with.

As for compositions not solely penned by Ian, "The Story Of The Hare Who Lost His Spectacles", with its contributions from Jeffrey Hammond and John Evan, adds a unique flavour to the list.

Outside of the top rankings, honourable mentions go to "Wondering Aloud" and "Budapest". And when it comes to standout performances, Martin's guitar solo in "Steel Monkey" earns top marks, while Ian's flute solo in "Locomotive Breath" remains a timeless favourite.

Undoubtedly, as you have read through this list, the tracks I have chosen and the order that I've put them in may have come as a surprise. It's true that tracks like "Aqualung", "Locomotive Breath", and "Bourée" are likely to be on most people's lists. However, song preferences are highly subjective, and rightfully so. My choices have been guided by personal taste, and everyone would undoubtedly have their own unique line-up.

Moreover, if I were to revisit this list tomorrow, next week, or even next year, I suspect "In Brief Visitation" would ascend to the top.

So, naturally, "Life Is A Longer Song: a Compendium of Another 33 1/3 Songs" will be my next project, exploring more of Tull's repertoire, from the popular to the obscure, the weird, and occasionally, the not-so-good. Just as Jethro Tull can do another Christmas song, I can certainly do another book.

In any evaluation of Jethro Tull, it's crucial to break away from the cliché that Ian Anderson alone is Jethro Tull, and vice versa. Numerous other individuals have made remarkable contributions along the band's journey, and they deserve a brief acknowledgment here as a tribute.

In the first line-up, Mick Abrahams didn't quite stand out with Tull but found success with Blodwyn Pig thereafter.

Glenn Cornick delivers a memorable bass solo on "Bourée" and anchors "Back To The Family" with his solid bass lines.

He sadly passed away due to heart issues in 2014. Clive Bunker's jazzy drumming shines on "Bourée", and he remains active in the music scene, occasionally collaborating with Martin Barre's band (more on that later).

Perhaps if ever Tull had a classic line-up, it was through the 1970s, with the odd change of bass player. John Evan was brilliant for Tull, as is evident in his arrangements, particularly for the intricate compositions of *Thick As A Brick* and *A Passion Play*.

Jeffrey Hammond-Hammond, known for his iconic zebra suits, was an underrated bassist.

Following him was Barriemore Barlow, whose drumming featured complex and innovative patterns that complemented Tull's music throughout the decade.

David Palmer played a pivotal role as Tull's main arranger in the late 1970s, particularly contributing to the folk trilogy of albums from *Songs From The Wood* to *Stormwatch*. Prior to his tragic passing at a young age in 1979, John Glascock was a remarkably fluid and intuitive bass player.

Dave Pegg, another underrated and understated bassist, remained loyal to Tull for fifteen years, despite the ongoing pull to return to Fairport Convention.

Eddie Jobson introduced the violin to Tull for just one album, with great effect. Mark Craney, another sad loss in 2005, drummed admirably on the A album.

Peter-John Vitesse, perhaps unfairly blamed by fans for the shortcomings of *Under Wraps*, brought youthful enthusiasm and virtuosity that revitalised the band in the early 1980s.

Gerry Conway was a superb drummer for Tull during that period and contributed to sessions for Tull later in the eighties, notably playing on the third of "Jump Start" featured in this book.

Gerry Conway sadly passed away on the 29th March 2024 aged 76. Before Tull in the seventies his main drumming role was with Cat Stevens, while later in the eighties he toured with Richard Thompson amongst others and then played with Fairport Convention for many years from 1998 to 2022. My own favourite Gerry drumming moment with Tull was on the song "Mayhem Maybe" from the box set of *Broadsword And The Beast* where he sounds like he is playing Irish Bodhran drums to brilliant effect! RIP Gerry!

Doane Perry joined in 1984, thankfully replacing the fiendish drum machine "Mr. A. Linn Drum". Perry could play anything in any style with a smile on his face.

Famous metal and rock keyboard player Don Airey joined Tull for some live tours in the mid-1980s, probably to give his hearing a bit of a rest. He currently resides in Deep Purple.

One of the nicest stories concerns Martin Allcock, who was the Fairport Convention guitar player but ended up as Tull's keyboard player in the late eighties and early nineties because he was a top bloke, fitted in well, and already knew Dave Pegg. He became another sad loss in 2018.

By the nineties, Andy Giddings had joined on keyboards as a virtuoso player and arranger. He was able to contribute to Ian's solo albums as well. Jonathan Noyce was a great bass player and had the added advantage of looking young enough to be Ian's grandson (only joking, but only just!).

By the mid-2000s, the current band was beginning to take shape. John O'Hara joined on keyboards, bringing another arranger who knew his way around a keyboard or two.

Dave Goodier handled bass duties, while Florian Opahle primarily contributed guitar to Ian's solo albums and tours, although he did play on most of *The Zealot Gene*.

Joe Parrish joined in time for *RökFlöte*. All of these musicians are great players and integral to modern-day Tull. Without them, who knows where the band would be?

In February 2024 Joe left Tull and was replaced by Jack Clark on lead guitar, who had played occasionally with the band before, as a bass player and second guitarist. He also plays guitar in Joe's folk rock band Albion. Having seen Tull just recently I can guarantee he definitely knows the riff to "Aqualung" and a few other songs besides. He is a worthy new addition to the band.

This brings us to the magnificent Martin Barre, Tull's guitarist from 1969 to 2011. In Tull, I always felt that Martin played with the song and for the song, rather than against it.

I once read an interview with Jethro Tull fan Ritchie Blackmore, who said he couldn't have been in Tull because he lacked the discipline that Martin had to play the complex arrangements for many of the songs.

Then there were the guitar solos, for which he is rightly lauded and recognised. "Aqualung" boasts one of the most iconic and easily recognisable solos of all time.

Finally, he has always come across as a thoroughly nice chap, being courteous, polite, and understated. He was very upset by the split in 2011. Nevertheless, he is now touring happily with his own band, playing Tull songs in unique arrangements to great acclaim. Long may that continue!

There are many others who have played the odd tour or just the odd gig with Tull, too numerous to mention here, who have also contributed to the band's history and majesty. Depending on how a full band member is interpreted and which accounts you read, there have been about twenty-eight members of Jethro Tull.

And so to Ian Anderson: at the last count, across studio and live performance contexts, as well as the flute, Ian has played acoustic guitar, electric guitar, mandolin, balalaika, harmonica, saxophones, violin, bass guitar, drums, tambourine, and portable crash symbols.

He has written the vast majority of the songs on his own and had the final say in production and arranging of the tracks.

He has run Jethro Tull as a commercial business for many years now. Ian Anderson is not Jethro Tull on his own, yet it is difficult to conceive of the band even remotely existing in the way that it has over the last fifty years without Ian being the dominant force.

It is a cliché, but is Ian, to all intents and purposes, Jethro Tull? He certainly is in the eyes of the public and many fans.

Where does Ian stand against other contemporary giants of the music world? He may not be as skilled a flute player as James Galway, nor did he invent jazzy, breathy flute playing (credit goes to Roland Kirk for that).

His singing might not rival the likes of Paul Rodgers or Bruce Dickinson, and he may never have penned a song as universally beloved as "Yesterday".

But the sum total of Ian Anderson is greater than the sum of his musical parts. What he has accomplished for Tull, and in his solo career, over fifty-five years, is the work of an absolute genius. And it's not over yet.

I am unabashedly a devoted Tull fan. This is apparent, some might say overly so. I'm also a bit of a "I know everything you never wanted to know about Tull" nerd.

However, I've endeavoured to present all this in the best possible taste in this book. While there are plenty of Tull songs I don't particularly care for, most of which have remained nameless, overall, I love Tull's music.

I've aimed to be critical, when necessary, yet maintain a positive tone. Additionally, I hope the humour sprinkled throughout has either helped or at least entertained.

Long may Ian and Jethro Tull continue! I eagerly anticipate the next album and tour. There's no reason why Ian Anderson and Jethro Tull can't continue for some time to come.

Here's an idea, Ian: how about a full theatrical Passion Play concert, with Marc Almond handling most of the vocals? You'd be on flute and everything else. Maybe Martin could even come back for that gig.

The Albert Hall could be a perfect venue for it, but failing that, my local village hall would do just fine. I'd even volunteer to make tea for the interval, right in the middle of "The Story Of The Hare Who Lost His Spectacles".

And that's it, the end of the book. And in the end, you can probably guess what the next line is...

"I'll pour a cup to you my darling. Raise it up, say Cheerio."

Bibliography
A bookend

For historical year by year "record, tour, band change", I used some of the excellent Tull Biographies out there, including:

Minstrels In The Gallery (David Rees)
Flying Colours: The Jethro Tull Reference Manual
(Greg Russo)

Both these books are quite elderly now, over twenty years old. They still serve to provide a plethora of information about the early years. The late 1960s and 1970s are well catered for with:

Jethro Tull Chronicles 1967-79 (Laura Shenton)
(very heavy, you will need a strong coffee table)

Original Jethro Tull: The Glory Years, 1968-80
(Gary Parker)

Unsurprisingly, the 1980s onwards are not as extensively covered, despite the fact there were still some great Tull times to be had. The main book is:

Jethro Tull... Into The 80s (Laura Shenton)

Books on Tull tend to overlook the 1990s and beyond. However, for a broader perspective, two upscale, beautifully illustrated volumes provide some factual background, touching on these later years:

The Ballard of Jethro Tull (edited by Mal Peachey)
Interviews by Mark Blake, where Ian and the
band speak (it's heavy: ditto the earlier coffee
table remarks)

Jethro Tull: Lend Me Your Ears (Richad Houghton)

A fan history (this one has my favourite Tull book cover).

The best resource for straightforward song information, covering both musical and lyrical aspects, is:

On Track Jethro Tull: every album, every track
(Jordan Blum)

This book thoroughly explores each Tull album and song up to *The Jethro Tull Christmas Album* in 2003. Jordan takes a scholarly and academic approach, providing formal music and lyrical analysis for every album and song until that year.

In contrast, I take a more informal and humorous approach, discussing and diverging from my selected songs.

Additionally, I've referenced several magazines that contain obscure yet fascinating factual titbits. These magazines include:

Record Collector Presents Jethro Tull
(September 2023)

Prog Rock: Jethro Tull (2018)

Jethro Tull: A New Day
Fan club magazine curated by David Rees and Martin Webb.
Numerous issues for the past forty years.

And last but not least:

The Ian Anderson-written sleeve notes that accompany every album and the excellently detailed booklets that come with the various Tull box sets.

Identifying the various websites used for research becomes a bit trickier now. This is where the Bibliography definitely becomes more selective!

Determining the total number of recorded songs by Jethro Tull was one of the most challenging factual aspects of writing this book.

As mentioned in the introduction, pinning down this number wasn't straightforward. Some websites suggested well over six hundred Tull songs, including live versions, while others offered various counts based on different criteria.

I used several websites and counted songs from albums, making educated guesses while acknowledging the limitations and potential inaccuracies, as highlighted in the introduction.

Similar methods were applied to estimate song numbers for other artists mentioned.

Fortunately, finding information on the number of concerts performed by Tull, Ian, Martin, and other bands was relatively easier. Two websites I relied on for this information were:

setlist.fm
ministry of information.com

For help with finding the song lyrics and their analysis, the two best sites were:

songfacts.com
songmeanings.com

For help with off-the-beat time signatures in chapter 3, I used:

soundbrenner.com

For chapter 12, to acquire some details about the use of accordions in rock and pop music, I looked at:

popmatters.com *41 essential songs that use accordions.*

To research the use of bagpipes in rock for chapter 16, I used:

loudersound.com *Bagpipes in rock.*

I also used various Tull-related sites and kept a beady eye on the Jethro Tull Facebook page. For everything else, as everybody else does, I predictably used:

Wikipedia! (but that is our little secret!)

Finally, I used myself as a walking, talking (nerdy) Tull encyclopaedia, but as I am not a book, magazine, box set or website, I don't count. It is definitely now time to bookend the bibliography.

About The Author

Richard Taylor resides in Essex with his wife Linda, inhabiting a house just large enough to accommodate his collection of 140 pieces of Jethro Tull memorabilia, spanning records, tapes, CDs, DVDs, box sets, programmes, magazines, fan club publications, and even sheet music.

While some may accuse him of being a nerdy Tull enthusiast, Richard maintains he enjoys other wholesome pastimes like table tennis, running, and watching cricket.

In addition to his hobbies, Richard volunteers as a radio presenter for a local community radio station, where he occasionally sneaks in the odd, or even good Jethro Tull track when nobody's looking.

This book marks his debut as a published author, although there are whispers of a second project in the works.